A JEWEL FOR ROYALS

(A THRONE FOR SISTERS -- BOOK 5)

MORGAN RICE

ISBN: 978-1-64029-333-5

Books by Morgan Rice

THE WAY OF STEEL
ONLY THE WORTHY (Book #1)

A THRONE FOR SISTERS
A THRONE FOR SISTERS (Book #1)
A COURT FOR THIEVES (Book #2)
A SONG FOR ORPHANS (Book #3)
A DIRGE FOR PRINCES (Book #4)
A JEWEL FOR ROYALS (BOOK #5)
A KISS FOR QUEENS (BOOK #6)

OF CROWNS AND GLORY
SLAVE, WARRIOR, QUEEN (Book #1)
ROGUE, PRISONER, PRINCESS (Book #2)
KNIGHT, HEIR, PRINCE (Book #3)
REBEL, PAWN, KING (Book #4)
SOLDIER, BROTHER, SORCERER (Book #5)
HERO, TRAITOR, DAUGHTER (Book #6)
RULER, RIVAL, EXILE (Book #7)
VICTOR, VANQUISHED, SON (Book #8)

KINGS AND SORCERERS
RISE OF THE DRAGONS (Book #1)
RISE OF THE VALIANT (Book #2)
THE WEIGHT OF HONOR (Book #3)
A FORGE OF VALOR (Book #4)
A REALM OF SHADOWS (Book #5)
NIGHT OF THE BOLD (Book #6)

THE SORCERER'S RING
A QUEST OF HEROES (Book #1)
A MARCH OF KINGS (Book #2)
A FATE OF DRAGONS (Book #3)
A CRY OF HONOR (Book #4)
A VOW OF GLORY (Book #5)
A CHARGE OF VALOR (Book #6)
A RITE OF SWORDS (Book #7)
A GRANT OF ARMS (Book #8)
A SKY OF SPELLS (Book #9)
A SEA OF SHIELDS (Book #10)

CHAPTER ONE

Sophia stared at the young man standing in front of her, and although she knew she should ask all kinds of questions, that didn't mean she doubted who he was for an instant. The touch of his mind against hers felt too close to the way it did with Kate. The look of him there in the sunlight was too similar.

He was her brother. There was no way he could be anything else. There was only one problem with that...

"How?" Sophia asked. "How are you my brother? I don't... I don't remember a brother. I don't even know your name."

"I'm Lucas," he said. He stepped down lightly onto the dock where she and Jan stood waiting. He moved with the smoothness of a dancer, the wooden slats seeming to give beneath each step. "And you're Sophia."

Sophia nodded. Then she hugged him. It seemed so natural to do it, so obvious. She hugged him tight, as if letting him go would mean him disappearing into thin air. Even so, she had to pull back, if only so that they could both breathe.

"I only found out your name, and Kate's, a little while ago," he said. To Sophia's surprise, Sienne was rubbing up against his legs, the forest cat twining close to him before pulling back to her. "My tutors told me when I came of age. When I got your message, I came as quickly as I could. Friends in the Silk Lands lent me a ship."

It sounded as though her brother had powerful friends. It still didn't answer her biggest question.

"How can I have a brother?" she asked. "I *don't* remember you. I didn't see your picture anywhere in Monthys."

"I was... hidden," Lucas said. "Our parents knew that their peace with the Dowager was fragile, and it would not withstand a son. They put about the story that I died."

Sophia felt herself staggering slightly. She felt Jan's hand on her arm, her cousin's touch steadying her.

"Are you all right?" he asked. "The child..."

You're pregnant? Again it felt different from when someone else with a spark of talent touched her mind. It felt familiar. It felt right, somehow. It felt like home.

1

I am, Sophia sent back with a smile. "But we should talk aloud for now."

She didn't know if Jan had known that her brother had similar powers to hers, but he did now. It seemed only fair to warn him of that, and give him a chance to guard his thoughts.

"And there are things that we should know," Jan said. He sounded suspicious in a way that Sophia wasn't, maybe because he hadn't felt that touch of mind. "How do we know that you are who you say?"

"You're Jan Skyddar, Lars Skyddar's son?" Lucas said. "My tutors taught me about all of you, though they cautioned me not to contact you until I was ready. They said that it would be dangerous. That you would not accept me. Perhaps they were right."

"He is my brother, Jan," Sophia said. She put the arm that Jan wasn't holding through Lucas's. "I can feel his powers, and… well, *look* at him."

"But there is no record of him," Jan insisted. "Oli would have mentioned it if there were a Danse *son.* He mentioned you and Kate enough."

"Part of hiding me was hiding the traces of me," Lucas said. "I imagine that they say I died as a babe. I don't blame you for not believing me."

Sophia blamed Jan a little, even though she understood it. She wanted this to be right. She wanted everyone to just accept her brother.

"We'll take him to the castle," Sophia said. "My uncle will know about it if anyone does."

Jan seemed to accept that, and they started to make their way back up through Ishjemme, past the wooden houses and the trees that sprouted between them. To Sophia, Lucas's presence seemed right somehow, as if a fragment of her life that she hadn't known was missing had somehow been returned.

"How old are you?" Sophia asked.

"Sixteen," he said. That put him midway between her and Kate, not the oldest, but the oldest boy. Sophia could see how that would have made things dangerous back in the Dowager's kingdom. Lucas going away hadn't kept *them* safe though, had it?

"And you've been living in the Silk Lands?" Jan asked. It had a note of interrogation to it.

"There, and a couple of places in their outer islands," Lucas replied. He sent an image across to Sophia of a house that was grand but flat, the rooms divided by silks rather than solid walls. "I thought it was normal to grow up being raised by tutors. Was it like that for you?"

"Not really." Sophia hesitated for a moment, then sent across an image of the House of the Unclaimed. She saw Lucas's, her *brother's*, jaw clench.

"I'll kill them," he promised, and maybe the intensity of that made him sit better with Jan, because her cousin nodded along with the sentiment.

"Kate beat you to it," Sophia assured him. "You'll like her."

"By the sounds of it, I'd better hope that she likes me," he replied.

Sophia had no doubts on that score. Lucas was their brother, and Kate would see that as clearly as she had. By the looks of it, the two of them were a good fit, too. They weren't the opposite poles that Kate and Sophia so often seemed to be.

"If you grew up… *there*," Lucas said, "how did you come to be here, Sophia?"

"It's a long and complicated story," Sophia assured him.

Her brother shrugged. "Well, it looks like a long walk back to the castle, and I'd like to know. I feel as if I've missed too much of your life already."

Sophia did her best, setting it out piece by piece, from escaping the House of the Unclaimed, to infiltrating the palace, falling in love with Sebastian, having to leave, being recaptured…

"It sounds as though you've been through a lot," Lucas said. "And you haven't even started to tell me how all this led to you ending up here."

"There was an artist: Laurette van Klett."

"The one who painted you, complete with the mark of the indentured?" Lucas said. He sounded as if he'd already placed her in the same category as the others who'd tormented her, and Sophia didn't want that.

"She paints what she sees," Sophia said. That was one person on her journey she held no anger toward. "And she saw the resemblance in a painting between me and my mother. Without that, I wouldn't have known where to start looking."

"Then we all owe her our gratitude," Jan said. "What about you, Lucas? You mentioned tutors before. What did they tutor you in? What did they tutor you to *become*?"

Again, Sophia had the sense of her cousin trying to protect her from her brother.

3

"They taught me languages and politics, fighting, and at least the beginnings of how to use the talents we all have," Lucas explained.

"They taught you how to be a king in waiting?" Jan asked.

Now Sophia understood some of his worry. He thought Lucas was there to try to push her aside. Honestly though, she suspected her cousin was more worried than she was. It wasn't as though she had *asked* to be called the heir to the throne of the Dowager's kingdom.

"You think I'm here to claim the throne?" Lucas asked. He shook his head. "They taught me to be a noble, as best they could. They also taught me that there is nothing more important than family. Nothing. It's why I came."

Sophia could feel his sincerity even if Jan couldn't. It was enough for her—more than enough. It helped her to feel… safe. She and Kate had relied on one another for so long. Now, there was her extended collection of cousins, her uncle… and a brother. Sophia couldn't say how much that felt as though her world had expanded.

The only thing that would make it better was Sebastian being there. That absence felt like a hole in the world that couldn't be filled.

"So," Lucas said. "The father of your child is the son of the woman who ordered our parents killed?"

"You think that makes things too complicated?" Sophia asked.

Lucas gave a kind of half-shrug. "Complicated, yes. Too complicated? That's for you to say. Why is he not here?"

"I don't know," Sophia admitted. "I wish he was."

At last, they arrived at the castle, moving through it to the hall. News of Lucas's arrival must have spread ahead of them, because all the cousins were there outside the hall, even Rika, who had a bandage masking the injury to her face she had received defending Sophia. Sophia went over to her first, taking her hands.

"Are you all right?" she asked.

"Are *you*?" Rika countered. "Is the baby?"

"Everything's fine," Sophia assured her. She looked around. "Is Kate here?"

Ulf shook his head. "Frig and I haven't seen her today."

Hans coughed. "We can't wait. We need to go in. Father is waiting."

He made it sound serious, but then, Sophia could remember what it had been like when she arrived there, and how cautious people had been with her. In Ishjemme, they were careful about people claiming to be one of their own. Sophia felt almost as

4

nervous standing there waiting for the doors to open as she had the first time, when it had been her claiming her heritage.

Lars Skyddar stood in front of the ducal seat, waiting for them with a serious expression as if ready to receive an ambassador. Sophia kept her hand interlinked with her brother's as she walked forward, even though that drew a frown of confusion from her uncle.

"Uncle," Sophia said, "this is Lucas. He's the one who came from the Silk Lands. He's my brother."

"I've told her that it isn't possible," Jan said. "That—"

Her uncle held up a hand. "There was a boy child. I thought... they told me, even *me*, that he died."

Lucas stepped forward. "I didn't die. I was hidden."

"In the Silk Lands?"

"With Official Ko," Lucas said.

The name seemed to be enough for Sophia's uncle. He stepped forward and treated Lucas to the same crushing, all-encompassing hug that he'd given Sophia when he'd recognized her.

"I thought I'd been blessed enough with my nieces coming back," he said. "I hadn't thought that I might have a nephew too. We must celebrate!"

It seemed obvious that there should be a banquet, and just as obvious that there was no time in which to prepare one, which meant that almost at once, there were servants running in almost every direction, trying to prepare things. It seemed almost that Sophia and Lucas became the still point at the heart of it all, standing there while even her cousins ran around trying to prepare things.

Are things always this chaotic? Lucas asked, as a half dozen servants ran past with platters.

Only when there's a new family member, I think, Sophia sent back. She stood there, wondering if she should ask the next question.

"Whatever it is, ask it," Lucas said. "I know there must be many things that you need to know."

"You said before that you were raised by tutors," Sophia said. "Does that mean... are my, *our*, parents not in the Silk Lands?"

Lucas shook his head. "At least, not that I could find. I've been looking since I came of age."

"You've been searching for them as well? Your tutors didn't know where they were?" Sophia asked. She sighed. "I'm sorry. I sound as though I'm not happy to have gained a brother. I am. I'm so happy you're here."

"But it would be perfect if it were all of us?" Lucas guessed. "I understand, Sophia. I have gained two sisters, and cousins... but I am greedy enough to want parents too."

"I don't think that counts as greed," Sophia said with a smile.

"Perhaps, perhaps not. Official Ko said that things are as they are, and pain comes from wishing otherwise. To be fair, he usually said it while drinking wine and being massaged with the finest oils."

"Do you know *anything* about our parents and where they went?" Sophia asked.

Lucas nodded. "I don't know where they went," he said. "But I know how to find them."

CHAPTER TWO

Kate opened her eyes as the blinding light faded, trying to make sense of where she was and what had happened. The last thing she remembered, she'd been fighting her way through to an image of Siobhan's fountain, plunging her blade into the ball of energy that had bound her to the witch as an apprentice. She'd severed the link. She'd won.

Now, it seemed that she was out in the open air, with no sign of Haxa's cottage or the caves that lay behind it. It looked only a little like the parts of Ishjemme's landscape that she had seen, but the flat meadows and bursts of woodland *could* have been there. Kate hoped so. The alternative was that the magic had transported her to some corner of the world she didn't know.

In spite of the strangeness of being in a place she didn't know, Kate felt free for the first time in a long time. She'd done it. She'd fought through everything that Siobhan, and her own mind, had put in the way, and she'd broken from the witch's grasp. Next to that, finding her way back to Ishjemme's castle seemed like an easy thing.

Kate picked a direction at random and set off, walking with steady steps.

She marched along, trying to think of what she would do with her newfound freedom. She would protect Sophia, obviously. That part went without saying. She would help to bring up her little niece or nephew when they arrived. Perhaps she would be able to send for Will, although with the war that might be difficult. And she would find their parents. Yes, that seemed like a good thing to do. Sophia wasn't going to be able to wander the world looking for them as her pregnancy progressed, but Kate could.

"First, I have to find where I am," she said. She looked around, but there were still no landmarks that she recognized. There was, however, a woman working a little ways away in a field, bent over a rake as she scraped away weeds. Perhaps she would be able to help.

"Hello!" Kate called out.

The woman looked up. She was old, her face lined with many seasons out there working. To her, Kate probably looked like some kind of bandit or thief, armed as she was. Even so, she smiled as Kate approached. People were friendly in Ishjemme.

"Hello, dear," she said. "Will you give me your name?"

"I'm Kate." And, because that didn't seem enough, because she *could* claim it now, "Kate Danse, daughter of Alfred and Christina Danse."

"A good name," the woman said. "What brings you out here?"

"I... don't know," Kate admitted. "I'm a bit lost. I was hoping you could help me to find my way."

"Of course," the woman said. "It is an honor that you have put your path into my hands. You are doing that, aren't you?"

That seemed an odd way to put it, but Kate didn't know where they were. Perhaps it was just how people spoke here.

"Yes, I suppose so," she said. "I'm trying to find my way back to Ishjemme."

"Of course," the woman said. "I know ways everywhere. Still, I feel that one turn deserves another." She hefted the rake. "I don't have much strength left these days. Will you give me your strength, Kate?"

If that was what it took to get back, Kate would work on a dozen fields. It couldn't be any harder than the tasks set in the House of the Unclaimed, or the more enjoyable work at Thomas's forge.

"Yes," Kate said, holding out her hand for the rake.

The other woman laughed and stepped back, pulling at the cloak she wore. It came away, and as it did so, everything about her seemed to shift. Siobhan stood there in front of her, and now the landscape around them changed, shifting to something far too familiar.

She was still in the dream space of the ritual.

Kate flung herself forward, knowing that her only chance lay in killing Siobhan now, but the woman of the fountain was faster. She flung her cloak, and somehow it became a bubble of raw power, whose walls held Kate as tightly as any prison cell.

"You can't do this," Kate yelled. "You have no power over me anymore!"

"I *had* no power," Siobhan said. "But you have just given me your path, your name, and your strength. Here, in this place, those things *mean* something."

Kate slammed her fist against the wall of the bubble. It held.

"You wouldn't want to weaken that bubble, Kate dear," Siobhan said. "You're a long way from the silver path now."

"You won't force me to be your apprentice again," Kate said. "You won't force me to kill for you."

"Oh, we're past that," Siobhan said. "Had I known that you would cause such trouble, I would never have made you my apprentice in the first place, but some things can't be foreseen, even by me."

"If I'm such trouble, why not let me go?" Kate tried. Even as she said it, she knew it wouldn't work like that. Pride would compel Siobhan to more, even if nothing else did.

"Let you go?" Siobhan said. "Do you know what you *did*, when you plunged a blade forged with my own runes into my fountain? When you carved apart our link, with no care for the consequences?"

"You didn't give me a choice," Kate said. "You—"

"*You* destroyed the heart of my power," Siobhan said. "So much of it, wiped out in an instant. I barely had the strength to hold to this. But I am not without knowledge, not without ways to survive."

She gestured, and the scene beyond the bubble shimmered. *Now* Kate recognized the interior of Haxa's cottage, carved on every surface with runes and figures. The rune witch sat on a chair, watching over Kate's still form. She'd obviously dragged or carried it up from the ritual space deeper in the caves.

"My fountain sustained me," Siobhan said. "Now I need a vessel to do the same. And there happens to be a conveniently empty one."

"No!" Kate shouted, slamming her hand against the bubble again.

"Oh, don't worry," Siobhan said. "I won't be there long. Just long enough to kill your sister, I think."

Kate went cold at the thought of that. "Why? Why do you want Sophia dead? Just to hurt me? Kill me instead. Please."

Siobhan considered her. "You really would give your life for her, wouldn't you? You'd kill for her. You'd die for her. And now none of that is enough."

"Please, Siobhan, I'm begging you!" Kate called out.

"If you didn't want this, you should have done as I required," Siobhan said. "With your help, I could have set things on a path where my home would have been safe forever. Where I would have had power. Now, you have taken that away, and I need to live."

Kate still didn't see why that meant Sophia had to die.

"Live in my body then," she said. "But don't hurt Sophia. You've no reason to."

9

"I've *every* reason," Siobhan said. "You think masquerading as the younger sister of a ruler is enough? You think dying in a single human lifetime is *enough*? Your sister carries a child. A child who will rule. I will shape it as an unborn thing. I will kill her and rip the child clear. I will take it and grow with it. I will become all I need to be."

"No," Kate said as she realized the full horror of it. "No."

Siobhan laughed, and there was cruelty in it. "They will kill your body when I kill Sophia," she said. "And you will be left here, between worlds. I hope you enjoy your freedom from me, apprentice."

She murmured words and it seemed that she faded. The image of Haxa's cottage didn't, though, and Kate found herself screaming as she saw her own body take a breath.

"Haxa, no, it isn't me!" she yelled, and then tried to send the same message with her power. Nothing happened.

On the other side of that slender divide, though, plenty happened. Siobhan gasped with her lungs, opened her eyes, and sat up with Kate's body.

"Easy, Kate," Haxa said, not rising. "You've had a long ordeal."

Kate watched her body feel around itself unsteadily, as if trying to work out where it was. To Haxa, it must have looked as though Kate was still disoriented by her experience, but Kate could see that Siobhan was testing out her limbs, working out what they could and couldn't do.

She finally stood, rising unsteadily. Her first step had her staggering, but her second was more confident. She drew Kate's sword, swishing it through the air as if testing the balance. Haxa looked a little worried at that, but didn't back away. Probably she thought it was the kind of thing Kate might do to test her balance and coordination.

"Do you know where you are?" Haxa asked.

Siobhan stared over at her using Kate's eyes. "Yes, I know."

"And you know who I am?"

"You are the one who calls herself Haxa to try to hide her name. You are the keeper of runes, and were no foe of mine until you decided to help my apprentice."

From where she stood trapped, Kate saw Haxa's expression shift to one of horror.

"You aren't Kate."

"No," Siobhan said, "I'm not."

10

She moved then, with all the speed and power of Kate's body, lunging with the light sword so that it was barely more than a flicker as it lanced into Haxa's chest. It protruded from the other side, transfixing her.

"The problem with names," Siobhan said, "is that they only work when you have breath to use them. You shouldn't have stood against me, rune witch."

She let Haxa fall, and then looked up, as if knowing where Kate's vantage point lay.

"She died because of you. Sophia will die because of you. Her child, and this kingdom, will be mine because of you. I want you to think about that, Kate. Think about it when the bubble fades and your fears come for you."

She waved a hand, and the image faded. Kate threw herself at the bubble, trying to get to her, trying to get out of there and find a way to stop Siobhan.

She paused as things around her shifted, becoming a kind of gray, misty landscape now that Siobhan wasn't shaping it to fool her. There was a faint glimmer of silver in the distance that might have been the safe path, but it was so far away it might as well not have been there.

Figures started to come from the mist. Kate recognized the faces of people she'd killed: nuns and soldiers, Lord Cranston's training master and the Master of Crows' men. She knew they were just images rather than ghosts, but that did nothing to reduce the fear that threaded through her, making her hand shake and the sword she carried seem useless.

Gertrude Illiard was there again, holding a pillow.

"I'm going to be first," she promised. "I'm going to smother you as you smothered me, but you won't die. Not here. No matter what we do to you, you won't die, even if you beg for it."

Kate looked around at them, and each of them held some kind of implement, whether it was a knife or a whip, a sword or a strangling rope. Each of them seemed to hunger with the need to hurt her, and Kate knew that they would fall upon her without mercy as soon as they could.

She could see the shield fading now, becoming more translucent. Kate gripped her sword tighter and braced herself for what was going to come.

CHAPTER THREE

Emeline followed Asha, Vincente, and the others across the moors beyond Strand, keeping hold of Cora's forearm so that they wouldn't lose one another in the mists that rose up off the moors.

"We did it," Emeline said. "We found Stonehome."

"I think Stonehome found us," Cora pointed out.

That was a fair point, given that the place's inhabitants had rescued them from execution. Emeline could still remember the burning heat of the pyres if she closed her eyes, the acrid stink of the smoke. She didn't want to.

"Also," Cora said, "I think that to find somewhere, you have to be able to see it."

I like your pet, Asha sent back, ahead of them. *Does she always talk this much?*

The woman who seemed to be one of Stonehome's leaders strode forward, her long coat trailing, her broad hat keeping off the damp.

She isn't my pet, Emeline sent over to her. She thought about saying it aloud for Cora's sake, but it was for her sake that she didn't.

Why else would someone keep one of the Normal around? Asha asked.

"Ignore Asha," Vincente said, aloud. He was tall enough to loom over them, but in spite of that, and the cleaver-like blade he carried, he seemed the friendlier of the two. "She has trouble believing that those without our gifts can be part of our community. Thankfully, not all of us feel that way. As for the mist, it is one of our protections. Those who seek Stonehome to harm it wander without finding it. They become lost."

"And we can hunt the ones who came to hurt us," Asha said, with a smile that wasn't entirely reassuring. "Still, we're nearly there. It will lift soon."

It did, and it was like stepping onto a broad island hemmed in by the mist, the land rising up out of it in a broad expanse that was easily bigger than Ashton had been. Not that it was packed with houses the way the city was. Instead, most of it seemed to be grazing land, or plots where people were working to grow vegetables. Within that perimeter of growing land sat a dry stone wall as high as someone's shoulder, sitting in front of a ditch in a way that made it into a defensive structure rather than just a marker. Emeline felt a faint flicker of power and wondered if there was more to it than that.

Within it, there sat a series of stone and peat houses: low cottages with peat and turf roofs, round houses that looked as though they had been there forever. At the heart of it was a stone circle similar to the others on the plain, except that this was larger, and filled with people.

They'd found Stonehome at last.

"Come on," Asha said, walking briskly toward it. "We'll get you settled in. I'll make sure no one mistakes you for an invader and kills you."

Emeline watched her, then looked over to Vincente.

"Is she always like this?" she asked.

"Usually she's worse," Vincente said. "But she helps to protect us. Come on, you should both see your new home."

They went down toward the stone-built village, the others following in their wake or breaking off to run to the fields to talk to friends.

"This seems such a beautiful place," Cora said. Emeline was glad she liked it. She wasn't sure what she would have done if her friend had decided that Stonehome wasn't the sanctuary she had been hoping for.

"It is," Vincente agreed. "I am not sure who founded it, but it quickly became a place for those like us."

"Those with powers," Emeline said.

Vincente shrugged. "That is what Asha says. Personally, I prefer to think of it as a place for all the dispossessed. You are both welcome here."

"As simply as that?" Cora asked.

Emeline guessed that her suspicions had a lot to do with the things they'd encountered on the road. It had seemed that almost everyone they'd met had been determined to rob them, enslave them, or worse. She had to admit that she might have shared a lot of them, except that these were people like her in so many ways. She wanted to be able to trust them.

"Your friend's powers make it obvious that she is one of us, while you... you were one of the indentured?"

Cora nodded.

"I know what that was like," Vincente said. "I grew up in a place where they told me I had to pay for my freedom. So did Asha.

She paid for it in blood. It is why she is careful about trusting others."

Emeline found herself thinking about Kate at that. She wondered what had become of Sophia's sister. Had she managed to find Sophia? Was she on the way to Stonehome too, or trying to find her way to Ishjemme to be with her? There was no way of knowing, but Emeline could hope.

They went down into the village, following Vincente. At first glance, it might have seemed like just a normal village, but as she looked closer, Emeline could see the differences. She could see the runes and spell marks worked into the stone and wood of the buildings, could feel the pressure of dozens of people with a talent for magic in the same space.

"It's so quiet here," Cora said.

It might have seemed quiet to her, but to Emeline, the air was alive with chatter as people communicated mind to mind. It seemed to be as common as talking aloud here, perhaps more so.

There were other things too. She had already seen what the healer, Tabor, could do, but there were those who were using other talents. One boy seemed to be playing a game of cup and ball without touching it. A man was sparking lights in glass jars, but there seemed to be no kindling involved. There was even a smith working without fire, the metal seeming to respond to his touch like a living thing.

"We all have our gifts," Vincente said. "We have collected knowledge, so that we can help those with power to express them as much as they can."

"You'd have liked our friend Sophia," Cora said. "She seemed to have all kinds of powers."

"Truly powerful individuals are rare," Vincente said. "The ones who seem strongest are often the most limited."

"And yet you manage to summon a mist that spreads for miles around," Emeline pointed out. She knew that took more than a limited stock of power. Far more.

"We do that together," Vincente said. "If you stay, you will probably contribute to it, Emeline."

He gestured to the circle at the heart of the village, where figures sat on stone seats. Emeline could feel the crackle of power there, even if it seemed that they were doing nothing more strenuous than staring. As she watched, one of them rose, looking exhausted, and another villager moved in to take their place.

Emeline hadn't thought of that. The most powerful of them got their power by channeling energy from other places. She'd heard of witches stealing people's lives away, while Sophia seemed to gain power from the land itself. That even made sense, given who she was. This, though… this was a whole village of those with power channeling it together to become more than the sum of their parts. How much power would they be able to generate like that?

"Look, Cora," she said, pointing. "They're protecting the whole village."

Cora stared at it. "That's… can anyone do that?"

"Anyone with a spark of power," Vincente said. "If someone normal were to do it, either nothing would happen, or…"

"Or?" Emeline asked.

"Their life would be sucked out. It is not safe to try."

Emeline could see Cora's discomfort at that, but it didn't seem to last. She was too busy looking around at the village as if trying to understand how it all worked.

"Come," Vincente said. "There's an empty house this way."

He led the way to a stone-walled cottage that wasn't very big, but still seemed more than big enough for the two of them. Its door creaked as Vincente opened it, but Emeline guessed that could be fixed. If she could learn to guide a boat or a wagon, she could learn to fix a door.

"What will we do here?" Cora asked.

Vincente smiled at that. "You'll live. Our farms bring in enough food, and we share it with anyone who helps work in the village. People contribute whatever they're suited to contribute. Those who can work metal or wood do it to build or to sell. Those who can fight work to protect the village, or hunt. We find a use for any talent."

"I've spent my life applying makeup to nobles while they prepare for parties," Cora said.

Vincente shrugged. "Well, I'm sure you'll find something. And there are celebrations here too. You'll find a way to fit in."

"And what if we wanted to leave?" Cora asked.

Emeline looked around. "Why would anyone *want* to leave? You don't want to, do you?"

She did the unthinkable then, and delved into her friend's mind without asking. She could feel the doubts there, but also the hope that this would be all right. Cora *wanted* to be able to stay. She just didn't want to feel like a caged animal. She didn't want to be trapped again. Emeline could understand that, but even so, she relaxed. Cora was going to stay.

"I don't," Cora said, "but… I need to know that this isn't all some trick, or some prison. I need to know that I'm not indentured again in all but name."

"You aren't," Vincente said. "We hope that you will stay, but if you choose to leave, we only ask that you keep our secrets. Those secrets protect Stonehome, more than the mist, more than our warriors. Now, I shall leave you to settle in. When you are ready, come to the roundhouse at the heart of the village. Flora runs the eating hall there, and there will be food for both of you."

He left, which meant that Emeline and Cora were able to look around their new home.

"It's small," Emeline said. "I know you used to live in a palace."

"I used to live in whatever corner of a palace I could find to sleep in," Cora pointed out. "Compared to a store cupboard or an empty niche, this is huge. It will need work though."

"We can work," Emeline said, already looking around to see the possibilities. "We crossed half of the kingdom. We can make a cottage better to live in."

"Do you think Kate or Sophia will ever come here?" Cora asked.

Emeline had been asking herself almost the same question. "I think Sophia is going to be busy in Ishjemme," she said. "With luck, she actually found her family."

"And you found yours, kind of," Cora said.

That was true. The people out there might not have truly been her kin, but they felt like it. They had experienced the same hatred out in the world, the same need to hide. And now, they were there for one another. It was as close to a definition of family as Emeline had found.

It made Cora family too. Emeline didn't want her to forget that.

Emeline hugged her. "This can be a family for both of us, I think. It's a place we can both be free. It's a place where we can both be *safe*."

"I like the idea of being safe," Cora said.

"*I* like the idea of not having to walk across the kingdom hunting for this place anymore," Emeline replied. She'd had enough of being on the road by now. She looked up. "We have a roof."

After so long on the road, even that seemed like a luxury.

"We have a roof," Cora agreed. "And a family."

It felt strange to be able to say it after so long. It was enough. More than enough.

CHAPTER FOUR

Dowager Queen Mary of the House of Flamberg sat in her receiving rooms and struggled to contain the fury that threatened to consume her. Fury at the embarrassment of the last day or so, fury at the way her body was betraying her, leaving her to cough blood into a lace handkerchief even now. Above all, fury at sons who would not do as they were told.

"Prince Rupert, your majesty," a servant announced, as her eldest son flounced into the receiving chamber, looking for all the world as though he expected praise for all that he had done.

"Congratulating me on my victory, Mother?" Rupert said.

The Dowager adopted her iciest tone. It was the only thing keeping her from shouting right then. "It is customary to bow."

That, at least, was enough to stop Rupert in his tracks, staring at her with a mixture of shock and anger before he essayed a brief bow. Good, let him remember that she still ruled here. He seemed to have forgotten it thoroughly enough in the past days.

"So, you want me to congratulate you, do you?" the Dowager asked.

"I won!" Rupert insisted. "I pushed back the invasion. I saved the kingdom."

He made it sound as if he were a knight riding back from some great quest in the old days. Well, days like that were long past.

"By following your own reckless plan rather than the one that was agreed," the Dowager said.

"It worked!"

The Dowager made an effort to contain her temper, at least for now. It was growing harder by the second, though.

"And you believe that the strategy I chose would not have worked?" she demanded. "You think that they would not have broken against our defenses? You think I should be proud of the *slaughter* you inflicted?"

"A slaughter of enemies, and of those who would not fight them," Rupert countered. "Do you think I haven't heard the stories of the things *you've* done, Mother? Of the killings of the nobles who supported the Danses? Of your agreement to let the Masked Goddess's church kill any they deemed evil?"

She would not let her son compare those things. She would not go over the hard necessities of the past with a boy who had been no more than a babe in arms for even the most recent of them.

"Those were different," she said. "We had no better options."

"We had no better options here," Rupert snapped.

"We had an option that didn't involve the slaughter of our people," the Dowager replied, with just as much heat in her tone. "That didn't involve the destruction of some of the kingdom's most valuable farmland. You pushed the New Army back, but our plan could have crushed it."

"Sebastian's plan was a foolish one, as you would have seen if you weren't so blind to his faults."

Which brought the Dowager to the second reason for her anger. The greater one, and the one that she'd been holding back only because she didn't trust herself not to explode with it.

"Where is your brother, Rupert?" she asked.

He tried for innocence. He should have realized by now that it didn't work with her.

"How would I know, Mother?"

"Rupert, Sebastian was last seen at the docks, trying to grab a ship to Ishjemme. You arrived personally to grab him. *Do you think I don't have spies?*"

She watched him trying to work out what to say next. He'd done this ever since he was a boy, trying to find the form of words that would let him cheat the world into the shape he wanted.

"Sebastian is in a safe place," Rupert said.

"Meaning that you have imprisoned him, your own brother. You have no right to do that, Rupert." A coughing fit took some of the punch from her words. She ignored the fresh blood.

"I'd have thought you'd be happy, Mother," he said. "He was, after all, trying to flee the kingdom after running out of the marriage *you* arranged."

That was true, but it didn't change anything. "If I wanted Sebastian stopped, I would have ordered it," she said. "You will release him at once."

"As you say, Mother," Rupert said, and again the Dowager had the feeling that he was anything but sincere.

"Rupert, let me be clear about this. Your actions today have placed all of us in great danger. Ordering the army around as you will? Imprisoning the heir to the throne without authority? What do you think that will look like to the Assembly of Nobles?"

"Damn them!" Rupert said, the words bursting out. "I have enough of them for this."

"You can't afford to damn them," the Dowager said. "The civil wars taught us that. We must work with them. And the fact that you talk as if you own a faction of them worries me, Rupert. You need to learn your place."

She could see his anger now, no longer disguised as it had been.

"My place is as your heir," he said.

"*Sebastian's* place is as my heir," the Dowager shot back. "Yours… the mountain lands require a governor to limit their raids southward. Perhaps life among the shepherds and the farmers will teach you humility. Or perhaps not, and at least you will be far enough away from here for me to forget my anger with you."

"You can't—"

"I can," the Dowager snapped back. "And just for arguing, it will not be the mountain lands, and you will not be a governor. You will go to the Near Colonies, where you will act as an assistant to my envoy there. He will provide regular reports on you, and you will not return until I deem you ready."

"Mother…" Rupert began.

The Dowager fixed him in place with a look. She could still do that, even if her body was crumbling.

"Speak again, and you will be a clerk in the *Far* Colonies," she snapped. "Now get out, and I expect to see Sebastian here by the end of the day. He is my heir, Rupert. Do not forget that."

"Trust me, Mother," Rupert said as he left. "I have not."

The Dowager waited until he was gone, then snapped her fingers at the nearest servant.

"There is still one more annoyance to be dealt with. Bring me Milady d'Angelica, then leave."

***

Angelica was still wearing her wedding dress when the guard came to her, summoning her to speak with the queen. He gave her no time to change, but merely escorted her briskly to her receiving chambers.

To Angelica, the old woman looked worn paper thin. Perhaps she would die soon. Just the thought of that had Angelica hoping that Sebastian would be found quickly, and made to go through with the wedding. There was too much at stake for it not to happen, in spite of the betrayal she currently felt at him running away.

19

She bobbed into a curtsey, then knelt as she felt the weight of the Dowager's gaze upon her. The old woman rose from her seat unsteadily, only emphasizing the difference in their positions.

"Explain to me," the Dowager said, "why I am not currently congratulating you on your wedding to my son."

Angelica dared to look up at her. "Sebastian ran. How was I to know that he would *run*?"

"Because you are not supposed to be stupid," the Dowager retorted.

Angelica felt a thrill of anger at that. This old woman loved playing games with her, seeing how far she could push. Soon, though, she would be in a position where she didn't need the old woman's approval.

"I took every step I could," Angelica said. "I seduced Sebastian."

"Not thoroughly enough!" the Dowager shouted, stepping forward to slap Angelica.

Angelica half rose, then felt strong hands pushing her down again. The guard had remained standing behind her, just a reminder of how helpless she was here. For the first time there, Angelica felt afraid.

"If you had seduced my son completely, he wouldn't have been trying to get away from here, to Ishjemme," the Dowager said, in a calmer tone. "What is in Ishjemme, Angelica?"

Angelica swallowed, answering out of reflex. "Sophia is."

That did nothing but stoke the other woman's anger.

"So my son was doing exactly what I told you to stop him from doing," the Dowager said. "I told you that the whole *point* of your continued existence was to prevent him from marrying that girl."

"You *didn't* tell me that she was the oldest daughter of the Danses," Angelica said, "or that they're claiming her as the rightful ruler of this kingdom."

This time, Angelica held firm for the Dowager's slap. She would be strong. She would find a way out of this. She would find a way to put that old woman on her knees before this was done.

"*I* am the rightful ruler of this kingdom," the Dowager said. "And my son will be after me. But if he marries her, that brings their kind in through the back door. It returns the kingdom to what it was, a place ruled by magic."

That was one thing Angelica could agree with her on. She had no love for those who could look into minds. If the Dowager could have seen into hers, no doubt she would have stabbed her simply as an act of self-preservation.

"I'm intrigued as to how you know all this," the Dowager said.

"I have a spy in Ishjemme," Angelica said, determined to show her usefulness. If she could show that she was still useful, this could still turn out to her advantage. "A noble there. I have been in contact with him for some time."

"So, you collude with a foreign power?" the Dowager asked. "With a family that has no love for me?"

"Not that," Angelica said. "I seek information. And… I may have already solved the problem with Sophia."

The Dowager didn't respond to that, merely left a gap into which Angelica felt she had to pour words before it claimed her.

"Endi has sent an assassin to kill her," Angelica said. "And I have hired one of my own should that fail. Even if he should reach there, Sebastian won't find Sophia waiting for him."

"He will not reach there," the Dowager said. "Rupert has imprisoned him."

"Imprisoned him?" Angelica said. "You must—"

"Do not tell me what I must do!"

The Dowager looked down at her, and now Angelica felt true terror.

"You have been a snake from the start," the Dowager said. "You tried to force my son into marriage by trickery. You sought to advance yourself at the expense of my family. You are a woman who hires assassins and spies, who kills those who stand against her. While I thought you might keep my son from his deluded attachment to this girl, I could stomach that. No more."

"It is no worse than you have done," Angelica insisted. She knew as soon as she said it that it was the wrong thing to say.

A nod from the Dowager, and the guard's hands were dragging Angelica roughly to her feet.

"I have only ever acted as I needed to in order to preserve my family," the Dowager said. "Every death, every compromise, was so that my sons would not be killed by someone else eager to seize power. Someone like *you*. You act only for yourself, and you will die for it."

"No," Angelica said, as if that one word had the power to stop it. "Please, I can make this right."

"You've had your chances," the Dowager said. "If my son will not marry you willingly, I'll not force him to bed down with a spider like you."

"The Assembly of Nobles… my family…"

"Oh, I probably can't truly have you wearing the mask of lead for your actions," the Dowager said, "but there are other ways.

21

Your fiancé has just abandoned you. Your queen has just spoken to you harshly. In retrospect, I should have seen how upset you were, how fragile…"

"No," Angelica said again.

The Dowager looked past her, to the guard. "Take her to the roof and throw her off it. Make it look as though she jumped from grief at losing Sebastian. Make sure you are not seen."

Angelica tried to beg, tried to fight her way clear, but already those strong hands were pulling her backward. She did the only thing she could, and screamed.

CHAPTER FIVE

Rupert stewed as he walked along Ashton's streets, toward its docks. He should have been riding down the streets to the cries of a loving populace, celebrating his victory. He should have had the common folk cheering his name and throwing flowers. There should have been women along the route eager to throw themselves at him, and young men jealous that they could never be him.

Instead, there were only damp streets and people going about whatever dreary business peasants got up to when they weren't cheering for their betters.

"Your highness, is everything all right?" Sir Quentin Mires asked. He walked as one of a dozen soldiers who had been chosen to accompany him, probably to make sure that he got to the ship without wandering off. Probably with orders to get Sebastian's location before he left. It wasn't even *close* to the same thing. It wasn't even enough for an honor guard, not really.

"No, Sir Quentin," Rupert said. "Everything is *not* all right."

He should have been the hero in this moment. He'd single-handedly stopped the invasion, when his mother and his brother had been too cowardly to do what was needed. He'd been the prince that the kingdom had required in that moment, and what was he getting for it?

"What is it even like in the Near Colonies?" he demanded.

"I'm told that their islands vary, your highness," Sir Quentin said. "Some are rocky, some are sandy, others have swamps."

"Swamps," Rupert repeated. "My mother has sent me to help rule over *swamps*."

"I'm told that there is a wide variety of wildlife there," Sir Quentin said. "Some of the kingdom's men of the natural sciences spend years there in the hopes of making discoveries."

"So *infested* swamps?" Rupert said. "You do know that you aren't making this better, Sir Quentin?" He decided to ask the important questions, checking things off on his fingers as he went. "Are there any good gambling parlors there? Famed courtesans? Notable local drinks?"

"I'm told the wine is—"

"*Damn the wine!*" Rupert snapped back, unable to help himself. Normally, he did a better job of remembering to be the golden prince that everyone expected. "Forgive me, Sir Quentin, but the quality of the wine or the plentiful wildlife will not make up for the fact that I am exiled in all but name."

The other man bowed his head. "No, your highness, of course not. You deserve better."

That was a statement so obvious as to be useless. Of course he deserved better. He was the elder of the princes and the rightful heir to the throne. He deserved everything that this kingdom had to offer.

"I've half a mind to tell my mother that I won't go," Rupert said. He glanced around at Ashton. He'd never thought that he would miss a stinking, squalid city like this.

"That might be... unwise, your highness," Sir Quentin said, in that special voice he had that probably meant he was trying to avoid calling Rupert an idiot. He probably thought Rupert didn't notice. People tended to think he was stupid, until it was too late.

"I know, I know," Rupert said. "If I stay, I risk execution. Do you actually think that my mother would execute me?"

The pause was too long as Sir Quentin searched for the next words.

"You do. You actually think that my mother would execute her own son."

"She does have a certain reputation for... ruthlessness," the courtier pointed out. Honestly, was this the way men with connections in the Assembly of Nobles talked all the time? "And even if she did not actually go through with *your* execution, those around you might be... vulnerable."

"Ah, so it's your own hide that you're worried about," Rupert said. That made more sense to him. People, he found, mostly looked after their own interests. It was a lesson he'd learned early. "I would have thought that your contacts in the Assembly would keep you safe, especially after a victory like this."

Sir Quentin shrugged. "In a month or two, perhaps. We have the support now. But for the moment, they are still talking about the overreach of royal power, about you acting without their consent. In the time it took for them to change their minds, a man might lose his head."

Sir Quentin might lose his anyway if he suggested that Rupert somehow needed permission to do what he wanted. He was the man who would become king!

"And of course, even if she did not execute you, your highness, your mother might imprison you, or send you off to a worse place with guards to make sure that you arrived safely."

Rupert gestured pointedly at the men who surrounded him, marching along in step with him and Sir Quentin.

"I thought that was what was happening already?"

Sir Quentin shook his head. "These men are among those who fought beside you against the New Army. They respect the boldness of your decision, and wanted to see that you did not leave alone, without the honor of an escort."

So it *was* an honor guard. Rupert wasn't sure that he could have taken it for one. Even so, now that he cared to look around at them, he saw that most of the men there were officers rather than common soldiers, and that most of them seemed happy to be accompanying him. It was closer to the kind of adulation that Rupert wanted, but it still wasn't enough to offset the stupidity of what his mother had done to him.

It was a humiliation, and, knowing his mother, a calculated one.

They reached the docks. Rupert had been expecting that for this at least there would be a grand fighting ship waiting, cannon firing a salute to him in acknowledgment of his status, if nothing else.

Instead, there was nothing.

"Where is the ship?" Rupert demanded, looking around. As far as he could see, the docks were merely bustling with the usual selection of ships, merchants getting back to their trade after the retreat of the New Army. He'd have thought that they, at least, would thank him for his efforts, but they seemed too busy trying to earn their coin.

"I believe the ship is there, your highness," Sir Quentin said, pointing.

"No," Rupert said, following the line of the other man's pointing finger. "No."

The boat was a tub, suitable for a merchant's journey, perhaps, and already partly loaded with goods for the journey back to the Near Colonies. It was anything but suitable to carry a prince.

"It is a little less than grand," Sir Quentin said. "But I believe Her Majesty thought that traveling without attention would lower the chances of danger along the way."

Rupert doubted that his mother had been thinking about pirates. She'd been thinking about what would make him the least comfortable, and she'd done a good job of judging it.

Still," Sir Quentin said, with a sigh, "at least you will not be alone in this."

Rupert stopped at that, staring at the other man.

"Forgive me, Sir Quentin," Rupert said, pinching the bridge of his nose to stave off a headache, "but why exactly are you here?"

Sir Quentin turned to him. "I'm sorry, your highness, I should have said. My own position has become… somewhat precarious at the moment."

"Meaning that you're scared of my mother's anger if I'm not around?" Rupert said.

"Wouldn't you be?" Sir Quentin asked, breaking free from the carefully considered phrases of the politician for a moment. "The way I see it, I can wait around for her to find an excuse to execute me, or I can pursue my family's business interests in the Near Colonies for a while."

He made it sound so simple: go to the Near Colonies, release Sebastian, wait for the furor to subside, and come back again looking suitably chastened. The trouble with that was simple: Rupert couldn't bring himself to do it.

He couldn't pretend to be sorry for something that had clearly been the right decision. He couldn't release his brother to take what was his. His brother didn't deserve to be free when he'd all but executed a coup against Rupert, using some ruse or trick with their mother to persuade her to give him the throne.

"I can't do it," Rupert said. "I *won't* do it."

"Your highness," Sir Quentin said, in that stupidly reasonable tone he had. "Your mother will have sent word to the governor of the Near Colonies. He will be expecting your arrival, and will send back word if you are not there. Even if you were to run, your mother will send soldiers, not least to find out where Prince Sebastian is."

Rupert barely, *barely,* restrained himself from hitting the other man. It wasn't a good idea to strike your allies, at least while they were still useful.

And Rupert had thought of a way that Sir Quentin could be *very* useful. He looked around the accompanying group of officers until he found one with blond hair who seemed to be around the right size.

"You, what is your name?"

"Aubry Chomley, your highness," the man said. His uniform had a captain's insignia.

"Well, Chomley," Rupert said, "how loyal are you?"

"Completely," the other man said. "I saw what you did against the New Army. You saved our kingdom, and you are the rightful heir to the throne."

"Good man," Rupert said. "Your loyalty does you credit, but now, I have a test of that loyalty."

"Name it," the other man said.

"I need you to swap clothes with me."

"Your highness?" The soldier and Sir Quentin managed to say it almost in unison.

Rupert managed not to sigh. "It's simple. Chomley here will go with you to the boat. He will pretend to be me, and go with you to the Near Colonies."

The soldier looked as nervous at that as if Rupert had commanded him to charge a horde of the enemy.

"Won't... won't people notice?" the man said. "Won't the governor notice?"

"Why would he?" Rupert asked. "I've never met the man, and Sir Quentin here will vouch for you. Won't you, Sir Quentin?"

Sir Quentin looked back and forth from Rupert to the soldier, obviously trying to calculate the course of action most likely to keep him his head.

This time, Rupert *did* sigh. "Look, it's simple. You go to the Near Colonies. You vouch for Chomley as me. Since I'm still here, that gives us a chance to get together the support we need. Support that could bring you back far quicker than if you start waiting for my mother to forget a slight."

That part seemed to catch the other man's attention. He nodded. "Very well," Sir Quentin said. "I'll do it."

"And you, Captain?" Rupert asked. "Or should I say General?"

It took a moment for that to sink in. He saw Chomley swallow.

"Anything you require, your highness," the man said.

It took a matter of minutes to find an empty building among the warehouses and the boat sheds, changing clothes with the captain so that now Chomley looked... well, frankly, nothing like a prince of the realm, but with Sir Quentin's recommendation it should be enough.

"Go," Rupert commanded them, and they went, accompanied by about half of the soldiers to make it seem more authentic. He looked around at the others, considering what he would do next.

There was no question of leaving Ashton, but he would have to move carefully now until he was ready. Sebastian was safe enough where he was for the time being. The palace was big enough that he would be able to keep away from his mother for a while at least. He knew he had support. It was time to find out how much, and how much power it could buy him.

"Come on," he told the others. "It's time to work out how we take what should be mine."

CHAPTER SIX

"I am Lady Emmeline Constance Ysalt D'Angelica, Marchioness of Sowerd and Lady of the Order of the Sash!" Angelica shouted out, hoping that someone would hear her. Hoping that her full name would demand attention if nothing else did. "I am being taken to be killed against my will!"

The guard dragging her didn't look concerned by it, which said to Angelica that there was no real chance of anyone hearing her. No one who would help, at least. In a place with as many cruelties as the palace, the servants were long used to ignoring cries for help, to being blind and deaf unless their betters told them not to be.

"I will not let you do this," Angelica said, trying to dig in her heels and hold her ground. The guard simply pulled her along anyway, the size difference too great. She struck out at him instead, and connected hard enough that her hand stung with it. For a moment the guard's grip relaxed, and Angelica turned to run.

The guard was on her in moments, grabbing at her and striking her so that Angelica's head rang with it.

"You can't… you can't strike me," she said. "People will know. You want to make this look like an accident!"

He slapped her again, and Angelica had the feeling that he did it simply because he could.

"After you've fallen from a building, no one will notice a bruise," he said. He snatched her up then, carrying her over his shoulder as easily as if she were a wayward child. Angelica had never felt as helpless as she did in that moment.

"Scream again," he warned, "and I'll hit you again."

Angelica didn't, if only because it didn't seem likely to make any difference. She hadn't seen anyone on the way here, either because everyone was still busy with the wedding that hadn't happened or because the Dowager had carefully kept them out of the way in preparation for this. Angelica wouldn't put that past her. The old woman planned as patiently and as cruelly as a cat waiting outside a mouse hole.

"You don't have to do this," Angelica said.

The guard replied with just a shrug that jostled her in her place on his shoulder. They went up through the palace, along winding staircases that narrowed more the further up they went. At one point, the guard had to set Angelica down just to get through, but he kept a cruel hold on her hair, dragging her along with a sharpness that made Angelica cry out in pain.

"You could just let me go," Angelica said. "No one would know."

The guard snorted at that. "No one would notice when you just popped back up at court, or in your family's home? The Dowager's spies wouldn't know you were alive?"

"I could leave," Angelica tried. The truth was that she would probably *have* to leave if she was going to live. The Dowager wouldn't stop at just this attempt on her life. "My family has interests so far across the sea that there's hardly ever news. I could disappear."

The guard didn't seem any more impressed by that idea than the last. "And when some spy mentions you? No, I reckon I'll do my duty."

"I could give you money," Angelica said. They were getting higher now. So high that, looking out of the slender windows, she could see the city arranged like some child's toy below. Maybe that was how the Dowager saw it: as a toy to be arranged for her amusement.

It meant that they must be almost at the roof, too.

"Don't you *want* money?" Angelica demanded. "A man like you can't earn much. I could give you enough wealth that you'd be a rich man."

"Can't give me anything if you're dead," the guard pointed out. "And I can't spend it if I am."

There was a small door ahead, iron bound, with a simple latch. Angelica thought that the route to her death should have more drama to it, somehow. Even so, just the sight of it made her fear rise again, making her pull back even while the guard dragged her forward.

If Angelica had possessed a dagger, she would have used it while he unlatched the door and opened it to let the cold air beyond rip at them. If she'd had so much as a sharp eating knife, she would have at least tried to cut his throat with it, but she didn't. In her wedding dress, she didn't. The most she had were a couple of powders designed to refresh her makeup, a sedative snuff that was supposed to be there for the threat of nerves, and… that was it. That was all she had. Everything else was below somewhere, tucked away against the conclusion of her wedding.

"Please," she begged, and there didn't have to be much acting to it to look helpless, "if money won't do it, then what about decency? I'm just a young woman, caught up in a game I didn't want. Please help me."

The guard pulled her out onto the roof. It was flat, with crenulations that had nothing to do with real defense. The wind whipped at Angelica's hair.

"Do you expect me to believe any of that?" the guard asked. "That you're just some innocent little thing? You know the stories they tell about you around the palace, milady?"

Angelica knew most of them. She made a point of knowing what people said about her so that she could have revenge for the slight later.

"They say that you're vain and you're cruel. That you've ruined people just for speaking to you in the wrong tone, and arranged for rivals to be shipped off with a mark of indenture tattooed on them where it wasn't before. You think you deserve mercy?"

"Those are lies," Angelica said. "They're—"

"I don't much care either way." He pulled her over toward the parapet. "The Dowager has given me my orders."

"And what will she do when you've fulfilled them?" Angelica demanded. "Do you think she'll let you live? If the Assembly were to find out that she murdered a noblewoman, she'd be deposed."

The big man shrugged. "I've killed for her before."

He said it as though it was nothing, and Angelica knew then that she was going to die. Whatever she said, whatever she tried, this man was going to murder her. By the look of it, he was going to enjoy it as well.

He pushed Angelica back toward the edge, and she knew it would just be moments before she fell. Inexplicably, she found herself thinking about Sebastian, and the thoughts weren't the hate-filled ones they should have been, given the way he'd abandoned her. Angelica couldn't understand why that would be the case, when he was nothing but the man she'd targeted as a husband to further her position, a man she'd been prepared to lure into bed with a sleeping powder…

An idea came to her. It was a desperate one, but right then, everything was desperate.

"I could offer you something more valuable than money," Angelica said. "Something better."

The guard laughed, but even so, he paused. "What?"

Angelica reached down to her belt, drawing out the small snuff box of sedative, lifting it as if it were the most precious thing in the world. The guard let her, staring almost entranced as he tried to work out what it was. Very delicately, Angelica opened the box.

"What is it?" the guard demanded. "It looks like—"

Angelica blew sharply, sending a scattering of powder into his face as he gasped. She cut left as he grabbed for her, hoping to dodge past while he was still dealing with the powder in his eyes. One meaty hand clamped on her arm, and the two of them pressed back toward the edge of the palace's roof.

Angelica didn't know what effect the sedative would have. It had worked quickly whenever she'd used it, but it was normally a thing of small doses and minor effects. How much would such a large dose do to a man that size, and would she have enough time before it happened? Already, Angelica could feel the edge of the roof against her back, the sky visible as the big man pushed at her.

"I'll kill you!" the guard bellowed, and the best Angelica could say about it was that his words came out slightly slurred. Was his grip weakening? Was the pressure pushing her back any less?

She was tilted back so much now that she could see the ground below her, and a scattering of servants and nobles. Another second, and she would be falling, to crash to the cobbles of the courtyard and smash as surely as a dropped goblet.

In that second, Angelica felt the guard's grip weaken. Not much, but enough for her to twist and slip by him, putting him with his back to the empty sky.

"You should have taken the money," she said, and charged forward, shoving with all her might. The guard teetered on the edge for a second, then toppled back, his arms flailing at the air.

Not just the air. One managed to catch at her, and Angelica found herself jerked forward, to the edge and over it. She screamed, grabbing for anything she could find. Her fingers found a piece of stonework, lost their grip, and then found it again while the guard continued to tumble below her. Angelica looked down just long enough to follow his fall to the ground. She felt a brief moment of satisfaction as he hit, quickly replaced by the terror that came from hanging from the side of the castle.

Angelica scrabbled for handholds, trying to find something more to hold onto. Her feet hung in thin air for a moment, then managed to find purchase on the rough sides of a stone-wrought heraldic shield. Angelica noted with faint amusement that it was the royal crest, but also couldn't help feeling relief at the fact it was there. Without it, she would undoubtedly now be as dead as the Dowager wished her to be.

The climb back up onto the roof seemed to take forever, Angelica's muscles burning with the unexpected effort. Below, she could hear screams now, as people started to gather around the fallen guard. No doubt, some of them would be looking up, seeing her as she made it back onto the roof, toppling over and lying there, breathing hard.

"Get up," she told herself. "You're dead if you stay here. *Get up.*"

She forced herself to her feet, trying to think. The Dowager had tried to kill her. The obvious thing to do was run, because who could stand up to the Dowager? She needed to find a way out of the palace, perhaps make it to the docks and set off for her family's lands overseas. That or sneak out through one of the city's smaller routes, avoiding any watchers that had been set and making it out into the country. Her family was powerful, with the kind of friends who could raise questions in the Assembly of Nobles over this, who would—

"They'll do what the Dowager tells them," Angelica told herself. If they acted at all, it would be so slowly that she would undoubtedly be murdered in the meantime. The best she could hope for was to run and keep running, never being safe, never being at the heart of things again. It was an unacceptable solution to it all.

Which brought her back to her earlier question: who could stand up to the Dowager?

Angelica dusted herself off carefully, rearranging her hair as neatly as possible as she nodded to herself. This plan was... dangerous, yes. Unpleasant, almost certainly. But it was the best chance that she had.

While the people below shouted, she set off at a run back through the palace.

CHAPTER SEVEN

Sebastian's eyes were starting to get used to the near dark of his cell, the damp, even the stench of it. He was starting to adjust to the faint gurgle of water somewhere in the distance and the sound of people coming and going beyond. That was probably a bad sign. There were some places that no one should get used to.

The cell was small, just a few feet on each side, with a front of iron bars, fastened with a solid lock. This was not some fine tower prison, where a man's family could pay for his upkeep in style until the time finally came for him to lose his head. This was the kind of place a man might be thrown into for the world to forget him.

"And if I'm forgotten," Sebastian whispered, "Rupert gets the crown."

That had to be what this was about. Sebastian had no doubt about that part. If his brother made him disappear, if he made it look as though Sebastian had run off never to return, then Rupert would become the heir to the throne by default. The fact that he hadn't killed Sebastian yet suggested that might be enough for him; that he might release Sebastian once he had what he wanted.

"Or it might just mean he wants to take his time about killing me," Sebastian said.

He couldn't hear other voices in the near dark at the moment, although from time to time they drifted in from further away. Sebastian suspected that there were other cells down here, maybe other prisoners. Wherever *here* was. That was actually a question worth thinking about. If they were beneath the palace somewhere, then there was a chance that Sebastian could attract enough attention to get help. If they were somewhere else in the city... well, it would depend on where they were, but Sebastian would find a way to get help.

He tried to think about the journey that they'd taken to get there, but it was impossible to say for certain. Not the palace, he guessed now. Even Rupert wouldn't be arrogant enough to stow Sebastian there. His brother, his family, had enough money that he could have bought other property around the city. Some extra house kept for liaisons or murky business.

"Probably both, knowing Rupert," Sebastian said.

"Shut up, you," a voice said. A figure came out of the dark: a nondescript man who served as one of his jailers. The man only came down a couple of times a day, bringing brackish water and stale bread. Now, he rattled a wooden club against the bars of Sebastian's cell, making him start at the sudden noise after so long in the silence.

"You know who I am," Sebastian said. "I'm Rupert's brother, the Dowager's younger son." He gripped the bars. "She will kill anyone involved in harming her sons. You know that, you aren't an idiot. Your only chance to survive right now is to be the one who lets me go."

Sebastian didn't like making the threat. It was the kind of thing his brother might have done, but it was also no more than the truth. His mother *would* tear Ashton apart looking for him if she thought that he'd been taken, and when she found him, anyone who had harmed him would die for it. When it came to her family, his mother was every inch the cruel, implacable monarch people believed.

"That only matters if she finds out," the guard said, swatting at Sebastian's hands almost casually with the club. Sebastian grimaced in pain, but managed to grab hold of the club, pulling the other man closer, his hands going to his belt.

It wasn't a good strategy. After all, the other man was armed, and Sebastian was trapped in a confined cell, without the ability to get around him, or avoid him. The guard struck him with his free hand, then jabbed him in the gut with his club. Sebastian felt the air rushing out of him. He went down to his knees.

"Arrogant nobles," the man snapped, spitting on the floor beside Sebastian. "Think that everything will work out for them, whatever they try. Well, it won't. Your mother won't come for you, you're not getting out of here, and I'll be standing right there when your brother decides to start cutting bits off you."

He hit Sebastian again with the club, then backed away into the dark. Sebastian heard the sound of a bolt.

He didn't mind the pain then, even though it ran across his ribs like fire. He didn't care about himself, or what Rupert might do, or what might be happening now to let all this take place. Even like this, Sebastian found his thoughts turning to Sophia, and Ishjemme, and his child.

How far along would her pregnancy be by now? Far enough that it would be visible; far enough that it wouldn't be so long until their child was born. Sebastian couldn't stand the thought that he might miss that moment, might miss hearing their child's first cries in the cold air of the dukedom. He couldn't stand the thought that he wasn't with Sophia now, standing by her side and protecting her from whatever harm the world tried to throw at her. He had no doubt that, once they learned that she lived, whoever had tried to kill her would make the attempt again. Sebastian needed to be there to stop it, whatever it took.

"Which is why," he said, taking out a key that he'd snatched from the guard's belt, "I need to escape."

Sebastian moved slowly and carefully, not wanting to make any more noise than he had to. He fit the key into the lock and managed to turn it, the grating sound of metal on metal seeming far too loud. The creak of the cell door was louder, sounding like it should summon guards at any moment.

Even so, Sebastian kept going. He edged from the cell, into the corridor beyond it. It was a short, cramped, dark corridor which, instead of a door at the end, had barrels, stacked up as if to hide the entrance to it. There were other cells too, set in a line, although for the moment at least, they were empty. Sebastian was grateful for that. He wasn't sure that he could escape himself without trying to take others with him.

Sebastian went to move the boxes and found that some of them were already set on a small wheeled cart, easy to push out of the way. It wasn't quite a secret door, but it served almost the same purpose. Sebastian pushed it aside, and now he could see that the corridor that held his cell was set back from a wide, vaulted cellar, lit with candles. Even the light from those was enough to sting his eyes after the dark.

He moved through the space carefully, looking at where butts of wine and casks of ale sat alongside beef, venison, and other supplies. A length of hard salt beef sat waiting to be consumed, and Sebastian tore off a hunk, chewing at it with the lack of grace of a starving man. He looked around, hoping to find, not a sword, because who would keep one of those in a cellar, but at least a carving knife or a butcher's hook. Something he could use in his escape.

There was nothing, and no time to hunt further. Sebastian didn't know how often people came through this space, and he needed to be gone before any of the guards got back. He hurried over to where a flight of stone steps led to a door, suggesting a way out. Sebastian hurried up those steps, ignoring the pain that came with each movement, and made it to the top.

He half expected the door to be bolted, but a door leading down to a cellar couldn't be, or how would people fetch things up for the house above? Sebastian was convinced now that it *was* a grand townhouse, and not the palace, simply because, as impressive as this space was, it didn't hold enough food to feed a whole palace of courtiers and servants, soldiers and nobles.

Sebastian swung the door open and found himself standing face to face with the guard who had beaten him, sitting on a chair, waiting for him. Two more men stood beside him.

"You thought I wouldn't notice my key was gone?" he asked. He laughed. "You think I would *carry* my key so close to you unless there were a reason?"

The truth seeped into Sebastian then, and the shock as it hit him made him stand there dumbly. They'd let him get this far. It was all some trick, some *game*.

"Do you think we don't watch the ones his highness tells us to?" the man said. "You think he hasn't had all kinds down there, trying to get out all ways? Oh, you should hear some of the women cry when they think they've escaped, neat as you like, only to be dragged back."

Sebastian threw himself forward at the man. It didn't matter in that moment that there were three of them, or that he was weak from the lack of food. What mattered was getting out of there, getting to Sophia, even if it hurt. He'd realized back at the wedding that he couldn't spend his life without her. Now was the moment when he proved it.

Sebastian's fist connected with the first man's jaw, making him stumble from his chair. His hand went down for his club, but Sebastian beat him to it, grabbing his wrist and holding his arm away from him. Sebastian struck out with his other elbow, slamming it into the guard's skull once, then again. The man went down, glassy-eyed, and Sebastian tumbled with him, not having the strength to keep his footing.

He scrambled to get up, and if he'd been at full strength, it might have been enough. He might have been away running into the house, searching for a weapon. As it was, a fist slammed into the side of his skull, and another struck him in the kidneys, sending agony through him.

Still, he fought back, kicking out at one of the remaining men, catching him on the knee. He pushed back to his feet, trying to turn and fight, throwing a punch that barely missed the last man.

They grabbed him then, working together with the kind of expertise that said they'd done it plenty of times before. These weren't soldiers who were used to fighting with blade or musket, just rough men who knew where to hit to cause the most pain, knew how to grab and hold so that Sebastian risked breaking his own arms if he continued to try to twist free.

They dragged him back toward the cell, and Sebastian fought more like a wounded animal than the prince he was supposed to be. He bucked and kicked, struck with his elbows and his head; anything so long as it would loosen the grip that never wavered on his arms.

"When Pellin wakes up, you're in for a kicking," one of them said. He sounded amused by the prospect.

"He might not wake up, the way this one hit him," the other said. He sounded just as amused by *that* idea. What kind of man liked the idea that his colleague, his friend, might die?

They dragged Sebastian back, all but throwing him down the stone steps, so that he tumbled and bounced, careening to the bottom. They picked him up again, dragging him to the cell and throwing him inside.

"Get used to it," one of them said. "It's not as though you'll be leaving."

The door shut with a clang that sounded far too final to Sebastian.

CHAPTER EIGHT

"You know how to find our parents?" Sophia repeated, wanting to make sure that she had the words right, barely daring to hope. She stared at her brother. Could Lucas really know that, when he'd already told her that he didn't know where they were?

"I know it sounds strange," Lucas said. "But I can find them. *We* can find them."

"How?" Sophia asked. Around her, the others in Ishjemme's hall seemed to be wondering the same thing. Her cousins and her uncle all leaned in as Lucas reached into the folds of the all-encompassing clothing he wore. Maybe a couple of them still thought that this might be a trick, and that he might draw a weapon after all. Sophia knew he wouldn't. This was her brother.

"Our parents knew they had to stay away from us to keep us safe," Lucas said. "And I think they knew that we were likely to find one another before we found them. Perhaps, given what they left, they even intended that you and Kate would be brought to the Silk Lands and raised with me."

Sophia thought that sounded too good to be true, but maybe it had been. Maybe her and Kate's nursemaid had known where to take them, before she'd sacrificed herself to save them. She knew that her parents would never have intended for her and Kate to end up in the House of the Unclaimed, so why was it so hard to believe that their destination might have been to end up with their brother?

"Why is that important for finding them?" she asked.

She saw Lucas draw something out of his clothes. It looked like a flat disc, or rather, like a series of copper and iron discs arranged in concentric circles. As her brother held it, Sophia saw lines glowing on its surface, with a power that seemed to have nothing to do with candles or lamps. Sophia could make out uneven lines, but couldn't see what they represented.

She could, however, make out the words that glowed around the rim: *Blood calls to blood.*

"What does it mean?" she asked.

"They have puzzle devices in the Silk Lands," Lucas said. "Arrange a box's lid the right way, and it will open, solve the puzzle of a disc like this, and it will show a picture. Official Ko employs an artist who makes puzzles that can show up to five different images, each more beautiful than the last."

Their uncle, Lars, leaned forward. "So if you twist that the right way, it will show us where Alfred and Christina hid themselves?"

"It hardly seems useful," her cousin Endi said from the side of the hall. "Even if you decipher it, it will only show where your parents were at the time they left it. You would have to go to find them after that."

Sophia suspected that there would be more to it than that. Just the glow coming from it said that it had a kind of power to it. Maybe it would be enough.

"If it's so easy," Lucas said, "solve it for us."

He tossed it to Endi, who caught it in spite of his surprise. As soon as he touched it, though, it was no more than a dull, flat circle of metal. The glowing lines were gone. Lucas held out his hand and Endi tossed it back. Lucas caught it with far more grace.

"If one of us touches it," he said, "it glows. I used to make a game out of it when I was small, running up to touch it when Official Ko wasn't watching, trying to get away again before he noticed the glow."

Sophia smiled at the thought of that.

"You think that it takes more of us touching it to make it work?" she asked. "You think it will take the three of us?"

In answer, Lucas held it out to her. "Let's find out. Perhaps I'm wrong. Perhaps two of us will be enough."

Sophia reached out for it, and as soon as she touched it, she could feel the power of the thing. Whoever had made it had managed to infuse something of her family's power into it, and even as she watched, that power started to have an effect. The concentric circles of the device started to move, grinding into place with strange clicks and whirs.

Sophia saw them start to form a picture, the lines coming together as the rings shifted. It took her a moment to make sense of them, but when she did, she saw the outlines of coasts and islands, rivers and roads snaking through them.

"It's a map," she said.

It was, but it was a map without a purpose. There was no mark suggesting where her parents might be, no clue to their location. It was the setting for an answer without its presence, and that was in some ways more frustrating than the unresolved puzzle had been.

Lucas seemed more optimistic.

"It is more than I have been able to do alone," Lucas said, "but not enough to find our parents. Perhaps if one can make this glow, and two can make it move, three will reveal the truth."

"We need Kate," Sophia agreed. She looked around. There was still no sign of her. "Has anyone seen her?"

That just brought shrugs and head shakes from her cousins. Frig stepped forward. "Ulf and I will find her, cousin. We'll send riders, and we'll go ourselves. She'll have gotten caught up hunting, no doubt."

"No doubt," Sophia said, although the truth was that she had at least *some* doubts. When Kate had been hunting in the last few days, she'd taken their cousins with her. "She'll want to hear this."

"And I'd like to finally meet *both* my sisters," Lucas said.

Sophia wondered how Kate would react to Lucas. She hoped Kate would like him as much as she did, would feel the same instant connection. She suspected that the two would have plenty in common.

"It will, at least, give us time to talk," her uncle, *their* uncle, said. "I'm sure Sophia wants to know more about your life with Official Ko. I know I do. How is the old man?"

"Older than ever," Lucas said. He laughed. "Fatter than ever, more careful in planning than ever, and more impossible."

"That sounds like Ko," Lars said. He obviously caught Sophia's questioning look, because he turned to her to explain. "Official Ko was the son of one of the Silk Lands' prefects when your parents and I met him. He had traveled here because he thought, almost uniquely for the Silk Lands, that there were things outside it worth learning. He arrived in the middle of the war, and when he left, I thought it must be because he had grown sick of it." He looked over at Lucas. "I should have guessed that he would have a purpose, and I am glad he did."

That seemed to be the cue for their cousins to dive in with their own questions.

"What is it like in the Silk Lands?" Rika asked. "They tell me that they have instruments there that play more beautifully than any harp."

"They have harpists too," Lucas said. "And from what I have heard of you, cousin, your playing is likely to be as beautiful as any there."

Rika flushed at that, and Sophia could pick out the pride in her thoughts, as the one cousin who couldn't shield them well.

"They say that your warriors can be formidable," Hans said. "Perhaps we could practice together some time."

41

"I would like that," Lucas said. There was something about the confidence with which he said it that told Sophia he didn't anticipate losing.

Sophia had her own questions. "Tell me more about growing up with Official Ko," she said. "What was it like?"

Lucas, her *brother,* paused for a moment, obviously thinking. "It was probably a strange life, looked at from outside," he said at last. "Even when I was small, I could see that not every child had a sword master to play fight with them, or a champion of the Far Steppes to teach them to wrestle. Official Ko brought in people to teach me everything from languages to calligraphy, and he would call me to his study every night to tell him what I had learned."

"That sounds like Ko," Uncle Lars said. "Did he try to teach you about this Virtuous Way of his?"

"The Way of Virtue, yes," Lucas said. He bowed his head. "I suspect that he was a better teacher than I was a student."

"All I know is that he was always drunk a lot for a man of so much virtue," Uncle Lars said.

Lucas smiled. "I asked him about that once. He explained to me that it was not about simple prohibitions, but about fitting in with the world, and his misfortune was that the world wanted him to drink wine."

They all laughed at that. Sophia was a little surprised by how quickly he'd managed to fit in with her family. He seemed to have the knack of getting on with people, which reminded her more of herself than of Kate. Lucas seemed to be somewhere between the two of them in more than just age.

"Official Ko must have taught you the arts of rulership as well," her cousin Endi said. "He must have tried to prepare you for what was expected of you."

"He did that part himself," Lucas said.

Sophia had to admit that she envied him that a little. When they'd told her who she was, and that it meant that she might one day be queen, it had felt as though she simply didn't know what she was supposed to be doing.

"I might have to ask you for tips," she said.

"I could be your advisor," Lucas suggested, in a tone that said he was only joking a little.

"Or Sophia could be yours," Endi said.

Sophia saw most of the others look at him in shock. Her uncle frowned.

"What do you mean, Endi?" Lars demanded. "Remember that we have sworn allegiance to your cousin."

Sophia saw Endi raise his hands in a gesture meant to placate.

"I'm not trying to cause any trouble," he said, "but we swore that before we knew that Lucas here was alive. Doesn't that make things complicated?"

"How would it make things complicated?" Jan asked, moving to Sophia's defense. "Sophia is to be queen."

She saw Endi nod. "Of course, of course. It's just... don't the old laws of the kingdom, don't *our* laws, say that it's the oldest *male* heir who inherits? Won't that cause problems building support?"

"Why would you try to cause a problem?" Rika asked.

Endi shook his head. "I'm not trying to cause problems, sister. I'm trying to *anticipate* them. What happens when our nobles start saying that Sophia should not be queen, because there is a king available? What happens when men do not fight for her banners? What happens when our forces splinter because half of them want to put Lucas on the throne?"

Sophia hadn't thought of it that way, but as soon as her cousin said it, she could see the potential problem. If she gave people any excuse to think that she wasn't legitimately their queen, wouldn't that make things more difficult? She wasn't sure what to think of that. It wasn't as though she'd ever set out to become queen. She just wanted to find her parents.

"Oli, what do you say?" Endi asked. "You know all the laws."

"Not all of them," Oli said, but Sophia knew that if anyone had been through the old law books, it would be her most studious cousin. "But in this case, I think you're right. I'm sorry."

He made it into an apology, but even so, it hurt. Sophia hadn't expected this to hurt. She'd never really wanted the role of queen in waiting, but now that they were threatening to take it away from her, it felt to Sophia as if she were losing the place where she belonged. She thought of all the disruption that this might cause, all the arguments...

She knew there was only one thing she could do.

Very carefully, she got down on one knee, looking up at her brother. "If they say that you're the one who should be king," Sophia said, "then you should be king, Lucas. If it will keep people safe, I will swear allegiance to you. You will be king."

And she... well, she didn't know what she would be.

CHAPTER NINE

Kate ran from the creatures that hunted her through the shifting darkness. She sliced with her sword as one got too close, but Kate didn't stop to try to fight it. She'd already found that some things couldn't be killed so easily.

The darkness around her changed, becoming the House of the Unclaimed. It was alight now, smoke burning in Kate's lungs, figures coming out of that smoke to grab for her. She recognized Sister O'Venn as the long dead masked nun swung a whip at her, the barbs of it slicing across Kate's skin in a flash of agony. She struck again as hands grabbed Kate's arms, dragging her toward the whipping post that sat at the center of the House's courtyard.

"No!" Kate yelled. "This didn't happen to me. It was Sophia you whipped!"

"Then you're long past due your turn, aren't you, you foolish girl?" Sister O'Venn snapped, lashing out once more with her weapon.

"This didn't happen," Kate said. "This isn't real!"

The pain was real, though, even if her skin healed the moment the lash was gone, even if there was no sign of the damage that it should have done. Kate might have been grateful for that another time, but here she realized the cruelty of it. It meant that there was no way for this to end, no promise of a release into death that might save her from more of it.

She screamed as they struck at her, the blows falling again and again.

Kate tore free, kicking at the images of the nuns. They shimmered as Kate struck them, revealing hints of other things underneath, things that made her mind refuse to look at them for fear of going mad. She didn't know whether they were fragments of her nightmares, things created by Siobhan to punish her, or simply the cruel inhabitants of whatever place her spirit occupied.

It didn't matter right then. What mattered was that she had to run, and keep running, even as the scene around her shifted again, and again.

How many times had it shifted so far? Kate wasn't sure that time worked the same way here as anywhere else. It felt as though she'd been here for days, suffering torment after torment, the horrors of her own mind coming at her, each with its own unique way of torturing her. Gertrude Illiard had come for her a dozen times, each with a new way to strangle or drown or smother her. The nuns followed with whips, the soldiers she'd killed with swords and knives.

Yet there were things here that tormented Kate in ways she couldn't have begun to imagine before this. There were creatures that clawed at her, masked torturers with brands and blades... Kate had screamed so much now that she should have been hoarse with it, but she wasn't, because even that didn't stop. There was still no cease, no way out.

"There *has* to be a way out," Kate said, pushing on through what seemed to be a jungle now, where every vine and branch had thorns to rip at her. There was the silver thread of the path out there somewhere, and if she could get back onto it, these things wouldn't be able to touch her.

That was easier said than done. There was no sign of the path that would keep her safe, no sign of a way out of this. Even as she ran, creatures sprang from the undergrowth, tearing at her with claws and teeth, the wounds ripping through her, gone as quickly as they came.

Kate could feel tears in her eyes, welling there and falling as the pain dragged them from her. She wept as she ran now, cursing herself for her weakness, but knowing that it didn't matter how strong she was. Without an end to the pain, the humiliation, the torture, this place would break anyone.

"You could stop fighting," Haxa said, the rune witch stepping up beside her then. They were in the caverns beneath her home now, the walls encrusted with runes and symbols, images and signs.

For a moment, Kate thought that she'd somehow managed to break free, springing back into the real world so that everything that had happened was just a dream. Then she remembered.

"You're dead," she said. "Siobhan murdered you."

"You killed me, as much as she did," Haxa said, and now her face twisted with anger in ways that no human face would have been able to. "You killed me the moment you set me against her. You killed me with your arrogance, your need to be free!"

"No," Kate said, backing away. "It wasn't me."

The runes on the walls began to twist, becoming red and angry things. Some of them reached out for her, wrapping her wrists in strands of power that held Kate as surely as any chains could have. Haxa stepped forward, and she had a knife in her hand.

"It's time we gave you a new name," the image of her said. Kate tried to tell herself that this wasn't the real witch, but it made no difference as the knife touched her, cut into her. Kate screamed as this version of Haxa started to carve runes on her flesh.

"Each one of these is the word for 'coward' in another language," Haxa said. "You are a coward, aren't you, Kate?"

Kate shook her head, but she was too busy screaming to speak.

"Oh, I know you were strong for a while with borrowed power, but that's just more cowardice. You needed what Siobhan gave you to feel safe. You abandoned your sister so you could seek it out."

"It wasn't like that," Kate managed.

"You sought to hide among a free company, knowing that they'd protect you," the twisted memory of Haxa accused as she continued to carve. "Then you ran from them when you knew the Dowager would send killers for you. You were too weak to refuse Siobhan when she wanted the merchant's daughter dead, then too much of a coward to obey her when she wanted you to do more for her."

"It isn't like that," Kate insisted. "You're twisting things."

The words hurt as much as any of the blades or the claws had. They tore at something deep inside of Kate, leaving her with no part of herself that she could keep safe from it all.

"You've twisted your whole life," Haxa said. "You've twisted it into a vile, cowardly mess that means no one will ever want you."

"Sophia," Kate said, through the tears. "Sophia has always been there!"

"Not for much longer. The woman of the fountain wears your flesh. So careless to leave it unguarded. Would you like to see what she will do with it?"

"No," Kate begged. "Please... no."

It didn't make a difference. What she wanted didn't matter here, only the things that would hurt her the most. Those seemed to be plucked from the innermost recesses of her soul in a never-ending stream. The air around her shimmered, showing Sophia and a figure that looked like Kate.

"How might she kill her?" the image of Haxa asked, only now it wasn't Haxa there. The face shifted from moment to moment, so that one instant it was a soldier talking, and the next it was Will. "Think of all the ways that she might slaughter your sister."

In the image, Kate saw a knife flash out, Sophia clutching her throat. It was so real that for a moment, Kate couldn't help herself.

"No!"

"Not that?" Now the creature in front of Kate wore her face. "How else should I do it? Let's see…"

Murder followed murder in the minutes that followed, the image of Kate attacking Sophia in ways that seemed inconceivable. She thrust a spear through her chest and strangled her with a cord, poisoned her drink and shot her with a musket. Each time, it felt as though Kate's heart was being ripped out.

She had to find a way to stop it; to at least warn her sister. Maybe there was a chance of that much, if nothing else. Kate pulled her power to her, ignoring the pain of her bonds, ignoring the images in front of her, ignoring everything except the need to find the connection that had been there since her birth. That connection had always been the one thing she had been able to reach for when she needed comfort or help. It had been inconstant, because she and Sophia hadn't always known how to use their powers, but Kate knew now.

She gathered up that power and threw it out in a simple call.

Sophia, you're in danger! I'm not who I appear to be! I'm trapped!

She threw the words out into the dark, hoping to feel the connection as she reached Sophia's mind. More than that, she hoped to hear words sent in response, coming back to her out of the silence she'd thrown them into.

There was nothing though. No answer, no connection, no hope.

"Oh, did you think you'd get out of here that easily?" the creature tormenting her demanded. It had claws now, and plunged them into Kate almost casually. "Defiance must be punished. Oath breakers must be punished."

"I'm not an oath breaker!" Kate yelled. She wrenched away, and now she wrenched away from her bonds, although something told her that it was only happening because she was being allowed to do it. She was being let free by the creatures in this place the way a cat might let a mouse go. Kate hated that image. She wasn't a mouse; she was a warrior!

"You're a killer," the voice said from the dark. "You're going to kill your sister, and they'll punish you for that. Siobhan will put you back into your body just in time to die. Would you like to see how they'll do it? Maybe they'll burn you like the witch you are."

Kate was running through a village now, but she stopped as she saw what lay ahead. A pyre sat there, seemingly made of body after body. Instinctively, Kate knew that it would be all the people whose deaths she'd caused. Instinctively, she shied away from that pyre, looking for another direction in which to run.

Hands grabbed for her, holding fast with the unyielding strength of the dead.

"Burn with us, Kate." a dead nun said.

"Don't you want to burn?" one of the New Army demanded.

Kate struggled to get away from them, but it seemed to make no difference. They dragged her forward, and now the pyre was alight, flames rising from it. The dead upon it screamed as they burned, their agony promising worse to come for Kate.

She wanted to call for help, but she couldn't think of anyone to call out to. Sophia couldn't hear her, and if she couldn't, then...

Maybe there was someone who could. There was someone who had heard her before, after all, hearing her cries for help even when Sophia hadn't been able to. Not knowing what else to do, Kate gathered up her power as the flames grew closer, throwing it out into the world.

Emeline, anyone, help me!

CHAPTER TEN

Cora stabbed at the earth with a hoe, surprised at how hard it was to break up simple clods of dirt. Already, she was sweating with the effort, and her hands felt raw. To her surprise, though, she was enjoying the work. She was enjoying the simple freedom of knowing that if she helped, this field would eventually produce food for all of them there. She was also enjoying the knowledge that she was doing this because she wanted, not because some noble had ordered her to.

"You're certainly getting the hang of this."

There were other things to enjoy about life in Stonehome, too. Aidan was one of them. He was working a little ways away, muscles moving beneath his shirt as he broke up the ground. His blond hair would have fallen to his shoulders if he hadn't bound it back with a strip of leather, pulling it away from some of the most handsome features Cora had seen. It was all she could do to not just stand there staring at him rather than working.

And now here he was, smiling at her.

"It's very different from helping people prepare for parties," Cora said.

"Well, maybe you'll have a chance to do that," Aidan said. "When the work is done with a field, the village likes to gather and celebrate. There's music, and dancing…"

"I don't really dance," Cora said. She'd always been the one watching the dancing from the sidelines, waiting for some noble girl or other to require repairs to her makeup, or some minor errand performed. "I've never learned how."

Aidan laughed. "I'm not sure dancing along to a fiddle is something you learn how to do. Besides, something tells me that you'd dance beautifully."

Cora could feel herself beginning to blush at that. She wasn't used to compliments. In her experience, generally people only complimented one another when they wanted something, and since she'd been indentured, they could always just take what they wanted from her.

"I don't know about that," Cora said, glancing away.

"At least promise that you'll dance with me and give me the chance to find out?" Aidan said.

Cora nodded, unsure what to say. Presumably, conversations like this one were ones where the majority of people got some kind of map to guide them through it. They were taught what to do by friends or families or others. They didn't have to stumble their way through, no one having thought that an indentured girl would need to know.

"What do you think of Stonehome so far?" Aidan asked.

"It's more than I could have imagined," Cora said, thinking of the mist that kept it safe, the incredible things that people there could do. "But it's different, too."

"I think people come here expecting a city," Aidan said. "That, or they think that they'll be waited on by servants. I'm guessing you didn't expect that though."

Cora shook her head, the absurdity of the idea almost making her laugh. "I was just hoping for somewhere I wouldn't be chased for being indentured," she said. "And, I guess, somewhere that I would fit in."

Even when he looked puzzled, Aidan was gorgeous. "You don't think you fit in here?"

"I do," Cora said. "It's just... this is obviously a place for people with gifts. I feel as though I'm being tolerated more than accepted. Does that make sense?"

She saw Aidan shrug. "I can understand it, but it doesn't mean that it's true. Everyone without a place to go is welcome here."

"But only the ones with magic can help to defend it," Cora said. "And those with magic are able to do the metalworking or the hunting with half the effort of anyone else. It leaves the likes of me hoeing fields."

She looked over to where the stone circle sat at the heart of the village. Emeline was there somewhere, contributing her part toward Stonehome's protection. She'd taken to her new home like a duck to water, fitting in as if she'd always belonged there, taking her turn at the stones, making new friends. Cora could easily imagine the day when her friend forgot who she was completely.

"It's normal to feel a little left out," Aidan said.

"That's another thing that's hard to get used to," Cora replied. "I always knew that Emeline and Sophia could read my mind, but now practically everyone can."

She blushed again at the thought of what Aidan might see if he looked into her mind. It wasn't as if she could just turn off everything that she was thinking about him. Worse, trying to stop just made thoughts of him spring instantly to mind, in all the most embarrassing ways.

"Don't worry," Aidan said. "I wouldn't read your thoughts… unless you wanted me to?"

"No!" Cora said hurriedly, and probably the speed with which she said it gave away far too much about the content of those thoughts. "No, I'd… maybe we could talk instead?"

Aidan smiled again. It was hard not to be distracted by that smile. "I'd like that. Or I could maybe show you a few ways you could play your own part in defending Stonehome?"

"I could do that?" Cora asked. From what she'd seen, it seemed to be mostly the province of those inhabitants with access to magic.

"Not the shield," Aidan said, "because trying to fuel that without magic would probably kill anyone who attempted it. Everyone needs to know how to fight, though, just in case someone makes it through the mist. We could work on that part. It might even help you to feel as though you fit in a bit better. People will like that you're making the effort to help try to protect them."

Cora nodded. She liked the sound of the idea. "I don't know if I'll be much of a fighter, though."

"You thought you couldn't dance, either," Aidan said. "I think I should demand proof of both."

He held out a hand and Cora took it, enjoying the feeling of her palm pressed into his as they moved off a little ways, to a space that had obviously been set up for exactly the kind of battle training Aidan had promised. There were weapons set in barrels under an awning, most of them looking quite old. Some of them looked as though rust was the only thing holding them together.

"These are just weapons for practice," Aidan said. "We trade for them, or we take them from hunters or bandits who come out onto the moors."

He picked out a pitted-looking musket, passing it to Cora. "Do you know how to load and fire this?"

Cora shook her head. No one had ever shown servants how to do that. Probably, they didn't want the indentured able to fight back.

"It's straightforward enough, but you have to be careful," Aidan said. "You need to work fast, too, because if an enemy is advancing, it can make the difference between getting a second shot, or not."

He started to show her the process of loading the weapon, measuring out the black powder and pushing home the wadding, setting a lead ball in the barrel and priming the firing pan. Aidan handed it to Cora, and she was surprised by the weight of it.

"You'll have to set your whole weight against it," Aidan said. "It isn't like a bow or a crossbow. It pushes back hard."

Cora pushed forward as she fired it. Even so, the kick of the weapon was enough to make her stagger back. She lost her footing and tumbled onto the grass. Aidan was there in an instant, helping her up.

"I'm so sorry," he said. "If I'd known—"

"It's fine," Cora said. "I want to be able to do this."

"OK," Aidan said, "but maybe we should work with the spear or the halberd for a while?"

Cora nodded, and they set to work with a long pole meant to simulate a spear. She found that suited her better, letting her slash and stab from a distance, while Aidan started to show her the proper way to set the thing against the ground, digging it in to receive the charge of a horse.

She'd been working at it for perhaps ten minutes when she saw a pair of figures approaching the training space. Emeline was walking beside Asha, the woman who was one of Stonehome's leaders. Emeline looked tired, even exhausted, after her stint at the stones. Cora was surprised she hadn't gone back to the cottage they were sharing if she was so utterly spent.

"Teaching the newcomer how to use a spear, Aidan?" Asha asked. "And I heard the musket. Wouldn't a hoe be more useful?"

"We all have to do our part to defend Stonehome," Aidan replied, in an even tone.

"That's true," Asha said. She looked over to Cora. "But the truth is that some of us can defend it better than others. Doesn't it make sense that *we* should focus on the fighting, while those whose talents lie in producing food or making clothes do that?"

It sounded to Cora like a recipe for another kind of nobility, ruling over another kind of indentured folk.

"You're not indentured here," Asha said, "and it's not about nobility. It's about everyone doing what they have the skills to do."

It took Cora a moment to realize that the other woman had read her thoughts. Apparently, not everyone there saw it as an invasion, the way Emeline or Aidan did.

"If you've nothing to hide," Asha said, "why worry about it?"

Cora didn't have a good answer to that, except that she didn't want people looking into her innermost thoughts, especially given everything she might be thinking about Aidan. Looking at Asha, she just *knew* that the other woman had seen that part, too. She decided to focus on the more important part.

"I think I should learn to fight," she said. "I might never be able to fight as well as some other people, but I can still do my part, and... well, how many people are exhausted at any one time from working in the stone circle? If people like me can hold back an attack, it gives them time to recover and join the fight."

"That's a fair point," Asha said. She didn't sound as though she wanted to admit it.

Emeline stepped in. "Besides, Cora is as brave as anyone you've met, Asha. She's traveled halfway across the kingdom with me, crossed rivers, stolen back our belongings from bandits, and more."

"Well then, maybe you're right. Maybe she should learn to fight. But not with that stick. Come on, you need to learn to fight with a sword. You both do. I was coming here to teach Emeline the basics anyway."

She picked out two practice swords, tossing them to Cora and Emeline. She seemed quite surprised when Cora caught hers neatly, determined to show Asha that she wasn't useless. Asha started to show them the basics of how to move with the sword, then quickly set them to fencing one another.

Emeline had some of the advantages, because she could pick out where Cora was going to move, but Cora was larger and stronger, while Emeline was obviously tired. They went back and forth, trading cuts and parries. Cora found that she was enjoying it a lot, especially when Aidan started calling out support from the side.

She saw Emeline freeze for a moment, and almost automatically, Cora's sword snaked out to touch her above the heart. When Emeline stayed there like that, Cora let the point drop.

"Emeline, are you all right?" she asked.

Emeline shook her head, looking like a sleeper coming out of a trance. She blinked at Cora as if only just seeing her for the first time.

"Are you all right?" Cora asked again. "Did something happen?"

"I thought I heard something," Emeline said. "Something... no, it's nothing. Shall we keep going, or should we go home?"

Home. Cora liked that word. She liked Stonehome too. Whatever else was true about it, it was her home now. And, she thought, looking over at Aidan, there were plenty of things to like here. She even liked the hard practice of the swordplay. She lifted her weapon again.

"What, when we still haven't worked out who the best warrior is?"

CHAPTER ELEVEN

The last time Rupert had met with those who supported him, there had been considerably fewer men there. Now, there were enough to crowd the dining room of the townhouse he was staying in, sipping port while they tried to pretend they had been with him all along, and had only been waiting to be asked. It was in the way of things that men were fickle.

"Gentlemen," he said, from a spot he'd chosen by the fireplace, "I am grateful to see so many men of note here. So many valiant soldiers, decisive members of the Assembly, and men of wealth."

That was true. What he was planning would only work if he had the soldiers, the law makers, and the men whose money moved the world around them. Rupert would have liked a couple of priestesses of the Masked Goddess there too, because those who had such a grip on the people's minds were important in their own way. But they were also prone to being his mother's creatures, and to moralizing against just about all of the things that Rupert found entertaining.

"Forgive me, your highness," one man, Lord Edgar Jarsborough, said. "But why is it that we are meeting here rather than in the Assembly of Nobles, or the palace?"

"Can a man not invite a few dozen of his closest friends for a gathering at his own home?" Rupert asked. It took the men there a moment or two to realize that they were meant to laugh at the joke, but once they did, they all took it up.

That would, of course, be the excuse to make it plausible to any watchers, because he'd hosted more than his share of debaucheries in the past. The truth, though, was simpler.

"The truth is that I cannot be seen in the open at the moment," he said. "It would place me in danger."

"Danger, your highness?" a captain wearing the colors of one of the free companies said. Rupert was surprised that he had survived the purge of them on the peninsula. Still, perhaps he could prove to be useful.

"Yes, danger," Rupert said. "As we speak, Sir Quentin Mires is heading to the Near Colonies with a young man playing the part of me, in an attempt to draw off any danger of an attack."

"But from whom?" Lord Jarsborough said. "Who would dare to attack your royal person, so soon after your victory against the kingdom's enemies?"

His victory; Rupert liked that he'd put it that way. But he didn't like the danger of this part, because this was the part where he had to tell these men the lie on which all the rest of it would hinge.

"My brother," he said.

Uproar followed, of course, as some men made noises that suggested such a thing was not possible, and others voiced their disapproval. Rupert waited for it all to die down as patiently as he could.

"Forgive me, your highness," Earl Astvel said, "but did you say that you are in danger from your brother? Prince Sebastian is a threat to your life?"

Rupert forced himself to nod gravely, mentally holding back the urge to curse the man for questioning him. He'd known that someone would. Men didn't know enough to simply accept the word of their betters these days.

"I'm sorry to say that he is," Rupert said. It was even true, in its way. Certainly, if their mother found out about what Rupert was currently doing to Sebastian, it might mean his death. "I know it is hard to believe."

Lord Jarsborough nodded. "Hard indeed, your highness. Prince Sebastian has acquired a reputation for loyalty, and for duty."

"Whereas I have acquired one for impetuousness, cruelty, and high-handedness," Rupert said. Had any of the men there said it, Rupert would already have been thinking of ways to avenge the insult, but for now, admitting it was useful. "Tell me, gentlemen, have any of you ever stopped to wonder *why* I have that reputation? I hadn't, until recently."

He looked around them, taking in the faces focused on him, the thoughtful looks. Sometimes he wondered what it must be like for other people, who didn't see the world as clearly as he did. Were they really that easy to control? He would find out in the next few minutes.

"I never asked myself why every childish folly of my youth was held up as evidence of evil, every attempt at proper decorum called aloofness. All I knew was that my every action was given the worst possible interpretation. When I tried to be brave, I was called reckless, and when I tried caution, I was named a coward. When I was generous, I was spendthrift, and when I held back, I became a cruel man with no charity. All the while, my brother, who acted in so many similar ways in private, was called dutiful and loyal, quiet and respectful."

Rupert paused, quietly enjoying this little twisting of the truth. It *was* only a small twisting, too, because as far as he could see, people had always been quick to judge his actions in ways they never had for his brother.

"If you want to know the truth of Sebastian, look at his behavior recently: trying to marry some unsuitable adventuress, then running away from a marriage into one of our most noble families not once, but twice. Disobeying orders in taking back rebellious islands. Proposing a coward's plan to save our kingdom that would have lost it."

That got some murmurs of assent from the men there, and Rupert resisted the urge to smile in triumph. Sebastian had given him all the ammunition he needed with his recent behavior. A year ago, this wouldn't have been possible. Now, it was all too easy to make Sebastian look like the villain of this piece.

"I had thought that wouldn't be a problem," Rupert said. "My mother has long made it clear that I am her heir, and Sebastian's behavior is something that can be tolerated. After all, he is my brother."

"Very magnanimous, your highness," Sir Audley Vilens, a prominent merchant, said.

"That was before Sebastian attempted to kill me when I was bringing him back home," Rupert said. "And before he started spreading rumors that he had been selected as our mother's heir." He gave it a moment before he said the next part. "Gentlemen, I believe my brother means to seize power."

Again, uproar, but again, Rupert had expected it. He stood back and let it wash over him, picking up key hints of it.

"…would restart the civil war…"

"…goes against everything we stand for…"

"…would leave us vulnerable…"

Rupert listened for a little while, and then decided that the moment had come.

"Gentlemen," he said. "I think we all agree that this thing cannot happen. That is why I am asking for your support. Sebastian has tried to get rid of me, and I have no doubt that his next move will be to arrange the death of our mother. We must seek to protect the Dowager, to secure Ashton, and the kingdom, against any threat of attack from within or without."

"What you're asking is dangerous," Sir Audley pointed out. "Those outside this might call this treason. Your mother—"

"Is that the same mother who has never given you lands of your own regardless of the amount of coin that goes into the royal coffers through your efforts?" Rupert asked. He turned to one of the soldiers there. "Is that the same mother who passed you over for promotion?"

He looked around them. "Who here has not been overlooked or put down by my mother?" he asked. "Whereas I am known to be generous to my friends. Help me do this, and the kingdom will be secure, while all of you will benefit. Allow Sebastian to tear it apart, and who knows what we all might lose?"

He watched them carefully, knowing that this was fragile, in spite of all he'd said. The men here didn't have any reason to like him. Indeed, many probably had reasons to hate him. They knew enough of him to know that his reputation wasn't entirely down to Sebastian's work. Ultimately, though, they were men of self-interest, and what had his mother ever done for them? For him?

Rupert waited as they came to their decisions. Lord Jarsborough was the first to speak, breaking the silence as he stepped forward.

"Very well," he said, with a bow. "I will aid you in this."

"And I," Sir Audley said, essaying a bow of his own. Neither man sounded excited by the prospect, but Rupert didn't need them excited. He needed them to obey, as they should do.

From there, it was a cascade of the others, none of them wanting to be the last to sign up for this grand conspiracy. Rupert waited until the last of them had bowed, trying to look the image of a dignified monarch in waiting, before he spoke.

"It is settled then," he said. "We act. For the crown!"

"For the crown!" the men repeated.

Rupert nodded. "Now, if you'll excuse me, there are things I must do, preparations I must make."

***

Rupert went down into the cellar, sliding aside the barrels that served as a false door. Normally, when he went down here, he felt a frisson of excitement at what he might do to those who had angered him, or made the mistake of catching his eye in the wrong ways. Today, he felt... strangely nostalgic.

"They tell me that you tried to escape," Rupert said. "You hurt one of my men quite badly, little brother."

He stared down at Sebastian. To his annoyance, his brother didn't look quite as broken and pathetic as he should have right then. Sebastian just wasn't good at playing the role that he was supposed to. Somehow, he managed to maintain a sense of dignity even in a cell.

"Do you care?" Sebastian shot back. "Do you actually care about anyone except yourself, Rupert?"

Rupert stood there, considering that question. As a general rule, he suspected that he *didn't* care about others in the way they professed to care for one another. He'd always seen that as a kind of lie people told themselves, or a game they played to fit in with the world. He'd never felt the need for it.

"Do you remember when we were little?" he asked Sebastian. "We would play at being soldiers together, out on the lawns of the country estates we visited."

"I remember that you took it as an excuse to thrash me," Sebastian said.

"Well, the idea was to win," Rupert shot back. He couldn't imagine playing a game like that and standing there, willingly letting his brother win. That would have meant a beating for *him*. "Do you remember the time Lord Greengage's children took it upon themselves to attack you?"

"I remember," Sebastian said.

"They'd surrounded you, I think," Rupert said. "Probably they were carried away with the game, or maybe they just saw a chance to hurt someone. People do, when they can."

"Not everyone," Sebastian insisted. He'd always been sentimental about that kind of thing.

"Do you remember that I stepped in?" Rupert asked. He could still remember charging toward them like some heroic knight out of history.

"You beat them senseless, you mean," Sebastian said. "I remember that. Are you going to tell me that I should overlook the part where you've locked me up because you saved me from some children, Rupert? Are you going to say that it shows how kind you are?"

Rupert shook his head. "It wasn't kindness. It was because you were *my* brother, and they didn't get to do that to you. You were *mine*. You used to run around, doing what I told you, but now you and Mother have gone and made things *complicated*. I'll have to deal with that, little brother."

"What are you going to do, Rupert?" Sebastian demanded, as if Rupert had any obligation to give him answers.

"For now," Rupert said, "I'm going to keep you here. It will be safer that way."

"Why not just kill me?" Sebastian asked.

Rupert cocked his head to one side. "Why would I do that? You can't do any harm here, and… well, it will give us a chance to talk."

To Rupert's surprise, he found that he quite liked that prospect. Rupert would go out and take a kingdom for himself while his brother would be here, waiting for him, whenever he wanted.

CHAPTER TWELVE

Sophia wasn't sure what to do. She'd never set out to be the queen of anywhere, but now that her cousins were telling her that she couldn't be, that Lucas should be king instead, she felt the pain of losing it.

For his part, her newfound brother watched her intently.

Are you all right?

His voice sounded in her head, sure and strong. Even that was a reminder, in its way, that he deserved this as much as she did. He had the same blood that Sophia and Kate did, and if he'd been the eldest, Sophia would have had no problem stepping aside.

I guess I don't like being passed over just because I'm a woman, she sent back.

Nor should you, Lucas replied. *I told you before how I stand on it.*

"I have no wish to be a king," he said, aloud so that her cousins could hear it. "Of the Dowager's kingdom, or anywhere else."

"But you are the oldest male heir," Oli said. Now that he'd been reminded of the rules, he didn't seem willing to let them go. Sophia didn't blame him for that; she knew how much her cousin doted on the rules of the past. She didn't even blame Endi, who she knew was only interested in protecting Ishjemme from the divisions that it might cause.

"But I am not the eldest," Lucas said, "and Sophia is the one who is suited to this."

"But you were raised to do this," Hans pointed out, "whereas Sophia… was not."

That annoyed Sophia a little. She turned to her cousin.

"I was brought up in a place that showed me what happens to the weakest in society when the strong do not defend them, Hans. Since then, I've seen the Dowager's court, and most of her land."

"In any case," Lucas said, "if there is one thing that learning with Official Ko taught me, it is that it is not enough to learn the five virtues and the sayings of the philosophers. I have the skills to aid a ruler, not to be one, whereas Sophia…"

He went down on his knee, offering up his sword in a movement so smooth it might have been rehearsed.

"I said this after I arrived," he said. "But I will say it again so that you can all hear. I do not wish to be king. Sophia will be queen, and I will serve her. I will defend her against all who would harm her... or try to take her throne from her."

"So will I," Jan said, from the side of the hall.

They came forward one by one, even Endi and Oli, who had raised it in the first place.

"Then the question becomes one of how we give Sophia back her throne," Hans said, when they were done. "Our army has been drilling, and now, when all the reports say that they are recovering from an attack, might be the perfect moment."

"Our armies are strong," Sophia's uncle said. He gave her a questioning look. "If this is the moment, then we could do a lot."

"This is one thing I could do for you," Lucas said. "I might not be cut out to sit on a throne, but I could take one for you."

Sophia could see how sincere they all were. Even Rika, whose mind seemed to be filled with fear at the thought, still didn't want to leave the Dowager on her throne when it could be Sophia instead. Looking at her, Sophia found herself thinking of the moment when a would-be assassin had almost killed her cousin while Rika tried to save Sophia.

She thought of all the people who would die in a war for the throne, on both sides. She wasn't naïve enough to believe that her army would sweep through Ashton without doing harm, or that there would be no risk to her family if they fought. What if she woke up one morning to find reports waiting for her that Lucas had been killed, so soon after finding him, or Kate...

...or Sebastian?

That was a thought that seemed like far too real a possibility. If there was an invasion, then Sebastian would be a target as one of the Dowager's sons. Sophia didn't want him having to run the way she'd run as a child. She didn't want him killed, just so that she could have a throne.

"I think you're all getting ahead of yourselves," Sophia said. "Why should we invade at all? You have a home that you love, and people to keep safe. I am more interested in finding my parents. Let's leave war to other people."

She wasn't sure if she was convincing them or not. That was the strange thing about talking to her cousins, where Rika was the only one whose thoughts she could read. The big difficulty was that Sophia knew this was an old argument, which they'd been having since before she arrived in Ishjemme. Most of the people of the dukedom had already decided what they thought.

"I still think—" Hans began, but he didn't finish it, because the doors to the great hall flew open. Sophia saw messengers rush in, and initially she thought that they might be bringing news of Kate, since riders had gone to look for her. Then she saw images in their thoughts of ships, and she knew the truth was far worse.

"We came... as fast as we could," one panted. "Ishjemme... I think we're under attack!"

***

Sophia could have waited safely within the walls of the castle, but some instinct told her that it was wrong to hide away while men were fighting, and maybe dying, for her. She didn't want to be the one who sat there scared in the middle of an attack. Instead, she hurried from the hall, her cousins trailing in her wake. Hans was shouting orders, gathering soldiers. Jan went to collect a sword and pistol. Her Uncle Lars was like the calm heart of it all, readying for war with the heavy certainty of experience.

"Tell me again what's happening," Sophia said to one of the messengers. "Tell me about the ships."

"They just arrived, your highness," one of the men said. "I don't see how they can have, though. They'd need to pick their way through the shallows, and to avoid being seen doing that... a man would have to know exactly where all the watchers were."

"Could they have been killed before they got a message back?" Lucas asked.

That was a worrying thought, and not just because Sophia hated the thought of men dying to try to protect their home. She hated the thought that they might have failed, and that, at any minute, enemies might descend on them.

"To do that," Hans said, "men would still have to sneak in without being seen. If even one were spotted, the towers would have lit their watch lights."

Still, Sophia couldn't think of another way for ships to just arrive in Ishjemme's harbor. With the amount of effort that it must have taken, she found herself wondering why they weren't already overwhelmed with enemies. Shouldn't the streets have been thick with them by now?

As they left the castle, Sophia could see the fjord spread out before Ishjemme, and she could see the dark ribbon of ships that sat there in it. Some of them looked battered, as if they'd just come from another fight, but there were enough of them that it didn't make a difference, especially not when they were turned broadside to bring their cannon to bear on the shore. Above them, dark specks circled.

"Crows," Uncle Lars said, in a tone that made it clear how much he hated the sight of them. "The New Army has come calling."

"Can we hold them back?" Sophia asked.

The hesitation before her uncle answered told its own story. They couldn't, and they knew it. Not like this.

"We've thought ourselves safe because the mountains make it hard to approach by land, and the watchers see those who approach by sea," he said. "Our armies are strong, but they aren't mustered for a battle. We could hold them back long enough to evacuate some of the population, and get them into the hills."

"Where they would starve," Sophia guessed.

Her uncle nodded. "Still, it may be the only option that we have."

Sophia wasn't so sure about that. There was something wrong about this situation, something that made no sense. This enemy was in a position to attack them, had made it past Ishjemme's defenses without effort, and yet they weren't pressing their advantage. The artillery that could flatten wooden buildings with ease wasn't firing. Soldiers weren't storming onto the docks.

The only sign of any advance from the forces was in the form of a trio of long rowing boats, out on the water. As Sophia watched, they rowed closer, though only one landed on the shore. Sophia was more interested in what the other two held.

"They have our men," Sophia said.

Ishjemme's watchers sat, hands bound, in the boats. Soldiers of the New Army surrounded them, armed and obviously ready to cut them down. The threat was clear.

"If we attack, they'll kill them," Lucas said, putting it into words.

Sophia looked around, half expecting to see Kate there, working through some plan to free them. But there was no sign of her sister. Where *was* she?

A man stepped from the boat that had landed. He did it alone, or almost alone. Crows came with him, riding on his shoulders as if they were pets, in numbers so thick they could have been a cloak. He was tall and slender, wearing a long frock coat that made him look a little like a particularly gentrified scarecrow.

"The Master of Crows," Lucas said. "It must be."

Uncle Lars had a stony expression. "A man with a musket could bring him down."

"And then our men would die, and his boats would attack," Sophia said. She heard his voice then, whispering in her mind like the rustle of wings.

Come to me. Speak with me alone, or your men will die one by one.

Sophia had no doubt that he would do it. She knew from Kate what he was capable of. Maybe it was just as well that her sister wasn't there, because there was no telling what she might have done in that situation. Actually, she suspected that she knew. Kate would have charged.

"He says that he wants to speak with me alone," Sophia said. As if on cue, the Master of Crows beckoned to her as if summoning her.

"Not alone," Lars said. "He'll kill you."

"If that were his plan, he'd just attack," Sophia pointed out. Sophia looked across to where the boats held Ishjemme's soldiers. "Besides, I won't ask them to die for me just because I'm too scared to risk this."

"Then we should all go down," Lucas said. "At least let me go with you."

"Or we attack," her uncle said.

Sophia shook her head. "You think a man who can guide ships here without being seen won't have planned for betrayal? You think those cannon of his won't fire? No, I have to do this. I *want* to do this."

She did. She wanted to meet this man who had fought with her sister, and whose army had caused so much misery. She wanted to know the enemy she might have to face.

"If I am your queen," she said, "then I have the right to choose to do this. If I am not, then I am not important enough to keep from doing it. Wait here. I'm going to talk with the Master of Crows."

CHAPTER THIRTEEN

Angelica arranged herself carefully in the chambers of Rupert's townhouse, considering how she would look from the door as precisely as possible, because she knew that she would only have one chance to make an impression. She sat carefully on the edge of a chair before his great bed, balanced in that very precise space between demure and desirable. She'd changed from her wedding dress, wearing a brand new affair taken from a dressmaker purely on the strength of her word. She hadn't dared to go back to her house yet, just in case the Dowager's men were waiting for her.

"She expects me to run and hide," Angelica whispered. "Well, I'll do neither."

"Talking to yourself, milady?" Rupert said as he entered. "You make a very poor burglar."

Angelica had to admit that he was handsome in his way. Perhaps more classically so than his brother, looking the way a prince was *meant* to. It didn't change anything about what lay underneath that exterior, of course, but it did potentially make some parts of this... easier. It was worth reminding herself of that.

"I'm not here to steal anything, your highness," Angelica said, her hands folded carefully. "I'm here to give you something. To offer you something."

Rupert's look held a note of expectation. "And just how did you even find me?"

That part hadn't been hard. Angelica knew all about Rupert's bolt holes. She'd thought that, once she married Sebastian, it might be useful to find him disgraced in one of them; possibly even dead in one of them, in time. She'd thought that it was prudent to know more about a man who might be her enemy than he wanted the world to know. Now, though, that knowledge had proven useful in trying to work out what to do in the wake of the Dowager's attack on her.

"Perhaps I just followed the trail of men of quality flocking to your door," Angelica said. "That was how I got in, incidentally. The servants were easy to convince that since you were seeking allies, I was one you might have invited."

"Seeking allies?" Rupert said. He frowned slightly, and with him, that was a dangerous expression. "You should be careful where you put your ears, milady, in case I decide to have them cropped."

Angelica made a point of not showing the fear that lay under the surface in that moment. She'd seen Rupert around the court. The only way to handle him was to match him perfectly, giving way so as not to spark his fury, but only after showing that you weren't weak enough to be beneath his contempt. It was the kind of balancing act that would have given a tumbler pause. Angelica needed to play it perfectly now.

"Is it so bad that I have heard?" Angelica asked. "Perhaps I'm exactly the kind of ally you need."

"The woman who was to be married to my brother?" Rupert shot back.

"The operative word there being 'was,'" Angelica replied. "And I'm also a woman your mother has no love for. Just as I'm told that her love for you has waned in recent months."

Rupert was there before her then, too close, his hand raised as if he might strike her. Angelica beat him to it, standing and slapping him so that he put a hand to his cheek.

"You *dare...*" he began.

"I dare that, and plenty else besides," Angelica said, not looking away, refusing to look weak in front of him. She brushed her fingers over the spot she'd struck, careful as a circus performer working with a barely tamed lion. "Besides, compared to the slap in the face of your mother picking Sebastian over you, we both know that's nothing."

"My mother did no such thing," Rupert said. "As I told the men who came here—"

"You told those fools what they needed to hear," Angelica said. "And from the look of them as they left, you did a good job of it. They'll never like you, but they'll rally to you rather than restart the war, or let your mother behave as she pleases."

"You make it sound as if I don't need you," Rupert said. He caught hold of her hand and squeezed. "It would be very bad for you if I didn't need you, right now."

"Oh, I'm sure you feel all kinds of need for me, my prince," Angelica breathed, ignoring the pain. "We'll get to that. For now, there's the part where my family has wealth and resources. Enough to support you in your rise to the crown. Enough to support you against our common enemy, if need be."

"My mother isn't my enemy," Rupert said.

Angelica raised one perfectly shaped eyebrow in a question. "Isn't she? Haven't you considered what she's done to you?"

"Perhaps," Rupert said, in a tone that suggested he'd thought it through a great deal.

"From what I hear, she tried to exile you in all but name. She'll hear you're back soon enough, and then? She probably won't call it imprisonment. You'll probably just be confined to one of your family's estates, or maybe here, but we both know what it will amount to."

Angelica took a breath, giving that a moment or two to sink in. The trick here was not to say all of what she wanted. She needed to guide Rupert in the right direction, and let him go the rest of the way himself.

"You'll stay there until you agree to serve Sebastian," she said. "She'll probably enjoy watching you bend your knee to him."

"I am already acting to deal with that," Rupert said.

Angelica shook her head. "By gathering a little support in the Assembly of Nobles? It's a start, but it won't be enough alone."

He cocked his head to one side. "What do you care, milady? I'd always taken you to be quite unfeeling about anyone but yourself."

"That isn't quite true," Angelica said. "There is at least one other person I care for."

She kissed him then, direct and sharp, catching Rupert unawares. He had some skill as a kisser once he recovered himself, but probably not as much as he thought. Or perhaps he just didn't care about anyone else's pleasure but his own.

"Are you going to try to tell me that you love me?" Rupert said. "When you've so nearly been married to my brother, twice?"

"If nobles only married for true love, you wouldn't have such an easy time seducing noblewomen from their husbands," Angelica pointed out. "We marry for power, or for bloodlines. Your brother was the one I thought I could get, when it seemed obvious that you would be married to some foreign princess. Your brother was *offered*."

"And you think I am for sale now?" Rupert demanded. He stepped back from her.

"I think that your mother has tried to kill me once, so I have no reason to listen to her decisions on the matter anymore," Angelica said. "I think I should marry the person with whom I *want* to spend my life."

It was a lie, but it was, she hoped, the right lie. Sometimes that was the best thing to hope for. She didn't want to think about what might happen if it proved to be the wrong lie.

"Because you're so desperately in love with me?" Rupert said. "You've rejected my advances before, Angelica."

"I had no wish to be some brief fling for you, discarded in the morning," Angelica said. "I don't want to be just another one of the women you use. I want to be your partner in all of this. I want someone beside me who will think as I do, and have the strength to act when it is needed. I want to share everything with you, my prince. My *king*."

She saw Rupert's expression change, caught with almost as much surprise as when she'd kissed him.

"Of course," Angelica added, "marrying me would bring considerable resources to your cause. My family has plenty of allies, enough to help secure a kingdom. For both of us, if we work together."

"You make a very persuasive point," Rupert said. Angelica could see him looking her up and down. "Very persuasive."

"Don't you want me, Rupert?" Angelica asked.

"Oh, very much," Rupert said. He moved closer to her, his hand twining in her hair... Angelica gasped as it jerked tight. "Tell me, though, is there any good reason why I should marry you for that, rather than taking what I want from you and finishing what my mother started?"

Angelica didn't squirm there. Instead, she held still, holding his gaze.

"Three reasons. First, you won't get anything my family has to offer if I'm not your bride. Second, I don't think you want to do what your mother wants right now…"

"And third?" Rupert prompted, with another painful jerk of his grip on Angelica's hair.

She moved quickly, taking a small knife from a fold of her dress and pressing it to the pit of his stomach.

"Because I'll gut you if you try," she said with a smile. She pressed forward, kissing him again then. "I've told you, Rupert. I understand you, probably better than anyone else here. I know what it's like, being surrounded by weak, stupid people. Do you want to throw away the one person who sees you for who you are and loves you for it? Your brother doesn't. He's fought you at every step. Your mother doesn't. She's trying to give away your throne. I will be there, beside you. Don't you want that?"

Rupert didn't hesitate. He kissed her hard. "Yes."

When he pushed her back toward the bed, Angelica barely remembered to get the knife out of the way in time.

Angelica lay beside Rupert, staring up at the painted plaster of the ceiling. He was asleep, in a way that was so predictable after everything that had happened between them in the last little while.

His lovemaking had been like his kissing: not quite concerned enough with her to be truly good at it, and just a little too rough for her tastes. Angelica knew that she would have to cover bruises with powder come the morning, but that was a price worth paying for everything she stood to gain.

A kingdom, security, revenge. Any one of them would have been worth this, but all three together would have been enough to make her give herself to almost any man. Rupert... well, asleep he looked like a sculptor's finest creation, and awake he was at least useful to her.

So why couldn't she stop thinking about Sebastian as she lay there? Even at the height of Rupert's efforts, it had been Sebastian's face she'd been picturing, and she'd had to make an effort to keep from crying out his name. Only the thought of what Rupert would have done to her if she had kept Angelica from doing it.

She pushed aside thoughts of Sebastian. He didn't matter now. She'd said it to Rupert: nobles like them didn't marry for love. Rupert was the brother she was going to marry, and who would give her the crown. More than that, with just the right touch, he was the brother who would give her the Dowager's fall for what she'd tried to do. That thought made her smile, and when she looked over at Rupert, she found him awake and staring at her.

"What has you so happy?" Rupert asked, in a surprisingly soft voice for him.

"You do, my love," Angelica said. Let him think of that what he would. It was even true in its way. Thanks to Rupert, Angelica would be safe from the Dowager's wrath. Thanks to Rupert, she would have the position she deserved at last. Thanks to Rupert, she would be queen.

That was worth smiling about, and more.

CHAPTER FOURTEEN

Sebastian sat in the dark of his cell, and it seemed to press in around him, reducing his world to the small sounds of the house above. There was the scrape of something that might have been a rat moving over stone, a faint drip of water somewhere that said it must have rained in Ashton. Even that small clue to the outside world felt like a precious gift to Sebastian, reminding him that there was something beyond the box of walls his brother had imprisoned him in.

He picked out other sounds too, as people moved through the basement that served to hide his cell. With an effort, he thought he could start to pick out the differences between the people who came to the basement: the heavy tread and loud jokes of the guards, the more hurried movements of the servants rushing to fetch and carry. Hearing those differences, Sebastian thought that he could see the beginnings of a plan taking shape in his mind. It was almost foolishly direct, but he couldn't think of another way right then.

He waited until the next time he heard a servant walking there alone, and called out, hoping that he was right, and that it wasn't just some guard with a lighter than average tread.

"Help! If you can hear me, this is Prince Sebastian! Can you hear me? This is Prince Sebastian! I am being held here against my will!"

He kept going, not knowing if it would work or if it would just bring violence down on his head from the guards. It was a dangerous move to try, because if he'd misjudged this, he was endangering any opportunity he had to try it again. If guards came, they would gag him, or find some other way of silencing him. Sebastian kept calling anyway; it was worth the risk.

For the next couple of minutes, he thought that nothing would happen. That even if somebody had heard him, they'd chosen to ignore him. It was obvious that Rupert would pick the kind of servant prepared to ignore calls for help from these cells. Sebastian could only hope that knowing it was him made a difference.

When he heard the creak of the barrels being pushed aside on their trolley, Sebastian dared to hope. A glimmer of light broke through and he saw a figure creep around the corner, holding a candle. It wasn't one of the guards. Instead, a young woman stood there, wearing drab servant's clothes, the hem of her dress high enough to show a mark of indenture.

"You shouldn't call out like that," she said, in a frightened voice. "If someone heard, it would cause trouble."

"I think I'm already *in* trouble," Sebastian said, with a gesture that took in his cell. "What's your name?"

The servant hesitated, obviously thinking about all the things that might happen to her if Sebastian revealed that name to anyone. "I… I'm Julia."

"Well, Julia," Sebastian said, "I'm Prince Sebastian, the Dowager's younger son. My brother is keeping me here against my will."

He suspected that all of that was obvious, but he wanted to be clear about it. He wanted to make it obvious what was at stake with all of this, and leave no room for doubt.

"I know," Julia said. She brushed a strand of dark hair back from her eyes. "I know who you are."

"Then you must also know that you need to help me," Sebastian said.

The young woman looked horrified at that prospect. "I can't," she said. "I *can't*. If they even find me talking to you like this, they'll put me in one of the other cells and… I heard someone's screams down here once. I *won't* end up here."

"No, you won't," Sebastian said. "I won't ask you to do anything that would put you in danger."

"I should go," Julia said. She glanced back toward the way out. "I was only supposed to be fetching wine."

Sebastian had the feeling that if she left now, she wouldn't come back. He had to stop her, and he could think of only one thing that would do it.

"Don't you want to be free?" he asked.

It was enough to make her stop, turning back to him. "Why would someone like you care about whether I'm free or not?"

Sebastian knew it was a fair question. It wasn't as though he'd spent his life trying to help every one of the indentured he could find. To her, he was probably just one more noble, trying to use her for his own benefit.

"Someone I love was indentured," he said. "I sent her away because of it. Now I'm trying to get back to her. If I can help other people like her along the way, I will."

The servant swallowed, obviously still thinking about the consequences for herself if she were caught.

"Then there's the other side of it," Sebastian said. "My mother will start tearing apart the city to find me soon enough. If I'm still here, that could put you in just as much danger as if you were caught helping me."

Sebastian didn't like trapping this young woman between the prospects of his mother and Rupert like that. Even so, it seemed to be what was required, because she nodded thoughtfully.

"I can't get you out of here," she said. "I don't have the keys. I couldn't steal them."

"I'm not asking you to," Sebastian said, trying to sound reassuring. "I just want you to take a message for me."

"To the palace?" the young woman said, looking just as horrified by that prospect. "They wouldn't let me in, and even if they did—"

"Not to the palace," Sebastian said. "I want you to take it to someone going in the direction of Ishjemme, or to someone who can send a bird there. The woman I love is there, and I think... I think she might be able to help."

"I don't know," Julia said. She glanced back toward the door. "They'll be calling for me soon. I have to go."

"Wait..." Sebastian called, but she was already leaving, darkness returning as the barrels moved back into place.

He sat there in the dark, not calling out when he heard the next set of feet. If he hadn't been able to convince someone who obviously had so much to gain from helping him, what hope did he have with anyone else? He spent his time trying to think instead, considering the ways that rescue might come for him. His mother might send people, learning about this place in the mysterious ways his mother seemed to learn so much else about the city. Someone involved in dragging him there might sell the information. Sebastian even had the brief hope that Sophia might come back for him, unable to live without him beside her, and find the location somehow.

He tried not to think about the more likely option: that he would sit there un-rescued until his brother decided that it was more convenient to simply kill him. If it came to that, Sebastian would fight. He would take any opportunity that arose to escape, but he'd already seen just how difficult that might prove. For now, he couldn't do anything but wait, and hope.

When he heard the sound of the barrels scraping back again, Sebastian found himself caught between that hope and the fear that he might have been found out. It wasn't fear for himself as much as it was for the servant he'd enlisted to help him. Had she been caught on her way out of the cellar? Had Rupert been there, and somehow guessed what had been happening there? Sebastian didn't want to think about what might happen then.

Yet, when the light flickered back into his view, he saw that it was Julia, carrying the stub of her candle, along with what looked like a scrap of paper and a short stick of charcoal.

"It's the best I can do," she said as she pushed them through the bars to Sebastian's cell. "Write your message, and I... I'll do my best to make sure that it gets to Ishjemme."

Sebastian had rarely written with tools so crude before, but right then, they might as well have been a gold-tipped quill and the blackest ink. All that mattered was that he had what he needed to get a message to Sophia, and tell her...

That was the hard part. There were so many words hemmed up inside Sebastian then that a whole sheaf of paper wouldn't have been sufficient for them, let alone this tiny scrap. He wanted to tell her how sorry he was for all the things he'd done, and how much he loved her. He wanted to tell her the things he dreamed for their future together, and how much he wished he were with her in Ishjemme. There was so little space, and so much he wanted to cram into it. Sebastian hunched close to the bars, working on the paper with his stub of charcoal by the candlelight, trying to write quickly, before they were discovered.

Sophia, my love, he wrote, *if this reaches you, know that I have tried all I could to get to you. I put aside my family, and tried to find a ship to Ishjemme, but my brother has seized me and locked me away in a townhouse in Ashton. Even if I never see you again, I want you to know that I love you more than life. Sebastian.*

He finished writing it and passed it to Julia, who tucked it away carefully in the folds of her dress, hiding it as well as she could.

"If this gets to her," Sebastian said, "she will be able to help us both. I know she will."

The servant nodded, although she clearly didn't share Sebastian's certainty. "I have to go," she said. "I didn't think it would take this long."

"I understand," Sebastian said. He took her hand through the bars. "Thank you, Julia."

She hurried away, taking the candle with her. Sebastian heard the barrels moving back into place. That was when he heard the one sound he'd been hoping he wouldn't: the heavier tread of a guard. He heard Julia's sound of surprise, and possibly pain, straining to hear the words that followed.

"What are you doing down here?"

Sebastian froze in fear at that voice, because it wasn't a guard's. Rupert's voice came through the walls, and even though Sebastian threw himself against the bars, there was nothing he could do.

"Cook sent me to fetch vegetables, sir," Julia replied. To Sebastian, the lie didn't sound very convincing, but maybe that was just his fears talking. The world seemed to hold still for a moment.

Then Julia shrieked in sudden pain.

"Do you think I'm stupid, girl? What do you have there?"

"No... please..."

There was another sound of pain, and then the scrape of the barrels, followed by the flare of a light. Rupert approached, holding the scrap of paper Sebastian had written his message on. He had blood on his hands as he tossed it contemptuously through the bars.

"The girl is going to suffer for your actions," Rupert said.

"This is my fault," Sebastian said, "not hers."

"And the best way to make you suffer is to hurt the people around you," Rupert shot back. "You care about them too much. Besides, I wouldn't hurt my own brother. Yet."

Sebastian threw himself at the bars, reaching through them to try to grab Rupert. His brother just laughed and stepped out of the way.

"I wonder, if I offered you your freedom now, would you take it?" Rupert asked. "What if I offered you your little accomplice too? Would you promise to leave and not come back?"

"Yes," Sebastian said. He even meant it. Let Rupert have the throne. He just wanted to get to Ishjemme to be with Sophia. He wanted the people who trusted him to be safe.

"I actually believe you," Rupert said. "But it doesn't work like that. You'll continue to rot here. This is your second lesson, brother. You won't like it if there is a third."

He turned and stalked away, ignoring Sebastian.

CHAPTER FIFTEEN

"Enough, enough," Emeline said, as she and Cora kept training. She stepped back, narrowly avoiding a blow from a training weapon, and raised her hands. "Keep going with Aidan if you want, but I'm exhausted."

She stepped over to the side, where Asha was waiting for her. The leader of Stonehome's fighters raised an eyebrow.

You're doing well, Emeline, but you shouldn't be losing to someone without your gifts.

I didn't lose, Emeline pointed out. *I'm exhausted, and anyway, if Cora is learning well, surely that's a good thing?*

Asha didn't reply, so Emeline turned her attention to where Cora was now practicing with Aidan again. Even without looking at her thoughts, Emeline could see just how happy Cora was to be around him. She was laughing as she fought now, and even though she was losing, because Aidan had been training much longer, Emeline could see her getting better with the light practice blade.

"If you don't have the strength for sword work," Asha said, "perhaps you'd like to learn to use your gifts more skillfully?"

"You could teach me to do that?" Emeline asked.

She saw Asha nod. "Some things are about affinity, talent, or knack, but many of them are just about the manipulation of power. You were able to give power to the stones, but there are other things you could do. Wiping away some of the thoughts of another, for example."

"That's possible?" Emeline asked. "But why would I need to?"

"Well," Asha said, "there's the matter of some of the things your friend is thinking about Aidan there being broadcast to the world. You could tone those down a little."

Emeline refused to be embarrassed. "Well, no one is making you read her thoughts."

"And no one is stopping me, either. With practice, she might be able to learn to defend herself that way, of course. But until then, it might be wise to have someone around who can manage what's there."

Emeline frowned. "You realize how that sounds?"

She would never be able to leave without it, Asha sent to her.

What?

The other woman looked at her. *I told you. Those who agree to keep our secrets can leave. But who can keep secrets if they can't protect their thoughts?*

"So you'd keep her here?" Emeline asked. "Or insist on wiping out her memory?"

"Only of our location," Asha said. "It would be for her protection as much as all of ours. She can't be tortured to give up what she doesn't know."

Asha made it all sound so reasonable, when to Emeline it sounded like the worst kind of theft. No, it was worse than that, it was like an assault on who someone was, a ripping apart of everything that made them themselves.

"Of course, there are other uses for such things," Asha said. "If you can touch the mind of another so strongly, you can shield their thoughts from intrusion, or fight off anything trying to control them. There are even those who can control them, though that kind of strength is rare."

Emeline smiled at that thought, because she'd seen the things that Sophia could do with her gifts. Asha seemed to take that as an invitation.

"It is easiest to feel this," she said. "Vincente is better at it, but I can show you. You will have to let me into your mind for this, though."

Emeline swallowed at that thought. She didn't like the idea of letting Asha in so soon after she'd talked about wiping memories. Even so, she lowered the protections that normally surrounded her mind.

"First, you must build the connection," Asha said, touching Emeline's mind. "Then you build a wall around someone's thoughts…"

Emeline felt her constructing it, felt the play of power there. Asha repeated it, once, then again.

"Now you," she said.

Emeline tried to copy the feeling of it, but it seemed to be more complicated than that. Her first attempt fell apart like smoke, while Asha shook her head at her second, pointing out the holes.

"I'm trying my best," she said.

"No, your best will be right," Asha said, unyielding as a rock. "Again."

Emeline sent her will out, locking it around Asha's mind, forming a shield that held as the other woman pushed at it.

"That's good," she said. "Now, let it go."

Emeline did so, grateful as she did, because she wasn't sure how much strength she had after working to give power to the stones for so long.

"To remove memories, you would wrap that shield around them and then you would pull it away, taking it with you."

She made it sound so simple, and so benign. Yet Emeline couldn't imagine doing it to someone, to Cora. It seemed as bad as stabbing them with a spear, or cutting off one of their hands.

"And if you could take away my memories of having to watch those two, I'd be grateful," Asha said, with a faint nod in the direction of Cora and Aidan.

They weren't practicing anymore. Instead, they were sitting on the stump of a tree together, talking. Then more than talking, as Emeline saw Cora lean in toward Aidan and kiss him, holding tight to him as she did it. Emeline looked away, but only to give her friend some privacy, not out of the kind of embarrassment Asha seemed to be suffering.

"Is it so bad to see people happy?" Emeline asked.

"No, it isn't," Asha said. "Are *you* happy here, Emeline?"

Emeline nodded. "It's different from how I imagined. There's so much focus on defending Stonehome."

"There are a lot of people who would see us all dead," Asha said. "Sometimes we have to be harsh, so that there is still a place where we can be safe."

She walked off, leaving Emeline to herself. She thought about going home herself, back to the little cottage near the edge of the community, so that she could leave Cora and Aidan to one another. As she looked back at them, they were still very much wrapped up in one another, still talking, still kissing, the two of them seeming to be unwilling to break apart. Emeline smiled and turned away.

A scream ripped through her mind, and Emeline realized that she hadn't put up the kind of defenses she normally would have in the wake of her lesson from Asha. The scream was horrifying in its pain and its fear. Worse, Emeline recognized the mind behind it, because she'd touched it before.

It was Kate.

Kate? Emeline sent, and for a moment she thought that perhaps she was mistaken. Her words seemed to drift out into the world, with nothing there to connect with. Then, with an agonized tinge that made Emeline recoil, more words poured into her mind.

Help! Kate sent to her. *I'm trapped. A witch has taken my body. She wants to kill Sophia.*

Sophia's in danger? Emeline sent back. *What is this? Where are you?*

Again, there was a pause that seemed too long before the next words came back.

Ishjemme. My body is in Ishjemme, but I'm not in it. I'm in a place... I don't know where it is. I don't even know if it's real. I came here to try to break my apprenticeship with Siobhan.

Emeline's breath caught at that. She could only guess at what space beyond the world Kate was caught in, and the sound of the witch's name filled her with fear. If Siobhan was hunting Sophia, then her friend was in real danger.

Save Sophia, Kate sent to her, *please. I can't contact anyone else. Save her. Save her baby.*

Her voice faded from Emeline's mind, and for a second or two, Emeline just stood there, not knowing what to do next. Yet there was only one thing she *could* do, wasn't there? Kate was calling her for help, and Sophia needed her help too. Emeline couldn't stand by and let anything happen to her.

Could she send a message to Sophia, warning her? Emeline couldn't see how. Unless Stonehome kept birds trained to seek Ishjemme, there would be no sending a message that way, and Emeline doubted that anyone there would have the power to send a mental message over that distance. That meant that any message she could send would travel at the speed of a courier, and would be far less certain than if Emeline did the obvious thing.

She walked over to Cora and Aidan, hating to interrupt them when they were just starting to get so close to one another. Even so, she needed to talk to Cora about this, and she needed to do it now.

"Cora, I'm sorry, but I need to talk to you. Sophia is in danger."

Cora looked around at her, and Emeline could feel her shock, but also her readiness. When it came to helping their friend, there was no hesitation.

"What? How? How do you know?"

"Her sister called out to me," Emeline explained. She explained about Kate's message, and about the danger the witch possessing her body posed to Sophia.

"We have to go to Ishjemme, then," Cora said, and Emeline could hear the determination there.

Emeline held up a hand. "Cora, maybe it's better if I go alone. We've only just found Stonehome, and you..." She glanced across at Aidan. "You've found so much here. I can save Sophia and Kate."

79

"What if you can't?" Cora asked. She sounded indignant then. "Emeline, do you really believe that, with my friends in danger, I'm going to let you go off alone?"

"I just thought—"

"Well, think again," Cora said. She turned to Aidan. "I'm sorry, but I have to do this. Without Sophia, I wouldn't be here. I'd still be in the palace."

Emeline watched as Aidan took her hand. "Then I think I probably owe her plenty, too. But do you know about what happens when people without powers leave?"

Emeline had the answer to that. "They take their memories of Stonehome. Asha was trying to teach me the technique while you two... sparred. They say you can't protect your thoughts from having the location taken."

"They'd take my memories?" Cora said. She looked at Aidan, and Emeline knew exactly which memories she was thinking of. It was one reason that Emeline had wanted to go alone.

"So maybe it's better if you stay," Emeline said. "I might be able to shield some of your thoughts, but I doubt they'd believe that I would be able to be with you all the time."

Cora stood there, looking from Aidan to Emeline, and Emeline could see the hesitation in her thoughts. She wanted to help Sophia. She wanted to go to Ishjemme, but she didn't want to risk forgetting about Aidan, and she didn't like the idea of having her memories taken.

"I'm still going," Cora said. "I'm not giving up my memories, though. Even if we have to sneak out, I'm not."

Emeline looked over to Aidan. "Will you keep our leaving secret for a few hours?" she asked. "I don't want to cause trouble for you, but—"

"It won't cause trouble for me," Aidan said, "because I won't be here. I'm coming with you."

Emeline frowned at that. "Are you sure that's a good idea?"

He shrugged. "I'm sure I'd rather be where Cora is, and who knows? Maybe with both of us there, Asha will believe that her thoughts were sufficiently protected."

Emeline wasn't sure it would work like that, because she'd seen how protective Asha was of her community. Emeline doubted that she would believe that Stonehome's secret was protected unless she saw Cora's memories taken. Even so, she was glad that Aidan was coming along, and not just because of the look of joy on Cora's face at the news.

When it came to fighting a witch powerful enough to defeat Kate, Emeline suspected that they were going to need all the help they could get.

CHAPTER SIXTEEN

Sophia felt as though she were walking to her execution as she made her way down the beach toward the Master of Crows. Sienne stalked beside her, but even that protection didn't seem like enough right then.

She put a hand over her belly protectively, thinking of what might happen to the child inside her if he chose to cut her down, but it wasn't just him she was afraid of. The boats out on the fjord still had their cannons turned in toward the shore, and could still fire at any moment.

Shall I make things more comfortable? he sent over to her. *The battles in the Dowager's kingdom have given me power to spare.*

He gestured, and the crows around him rose. He opened his coat, and more poured from it, joining with the others, until the space around him was black with them. They beat their wings, and the sand around Sophia rose up in answer to it, the dust forming a cloud that turned the rest of the world into shadows.

"I got the idea from something your sister did to my men," he said, as Sophia got close to him. His tone was oddly formal, while his accent sounded like something that had been preserved from an earlier time. "Of course, when she summoned mist, she killed them in it."

The fear within Sophia spiked at the threat contained in that, and she fought to push it back down. She put a restraining hand on Sienne's head as the forest cat growled.

"If you'd wanted to kill me, you would just have attacked," Sophia said, hoping it was true.

The Master of Crows regarded her the way one of his creatures might have looked at something, his head shifting slightly from side to side as if to get a better look.

"Perhaps I just wanted to make sure you wouldn't run," he said. "Perhaps I'm more interested in letting the crows feast on you than in this little dukedom."

"And are you?" Sophia asked. She looked around for a way to get clear if all this went wrong, but around her, all she could see was the swirling dust from the beach. It wasn't even possible to see which way led back to the others.

That was bad, because she doubted that she could fight a man like this one. He was taller, stronger, and not weighed down with months of pregnancy, even without taking into account the part where he was well armed and Sophia had no more than an eating knife. Sienne might make a difference, but Sophia didn't want to sacrifice the forest cat's life just so she could save herself.

"Not yet," he said, with a smile so brief it was barely there. "The crows will be fed better by you being alive. You will give them so many deaths, Sophia Danse, and each one will make me stronger."

Did he think that the use of her name would intimidate her? Sophia stood up tall, facing him down the way she'd faced down everyone from rude noblewomen to bandits.

"You don't get to decide what I do," she said.

"Don't I?"

She shook her head. "You're making the mistake that some of the nobles here are making. That even my cousins are making. You think I have an interest in going back to the Dowager's kingdom. You think I'm going to bring death and destruction to it for the sake of a throne I have never sought. I won't do it. I'm going to find my parents instead. I'd say I'm sorry to disappoint you, but I'm not."

The Master of Crows didn't seem perturbed by that. He stood there with a faint, knowing smile.

"You say that, and yet I can see the path ahead of you as clearly as if you have already walked it," he said. "The crows let me see a long way."

"Not far enough," Sophia said. Briefly, she wondered what it must be like to be something like that, so powerful that it turned him into something that wasn't even close to being human. She looked across to Sienne and wondered if she was on the start of the same path, and where it might lead if she were.

Then she realized that she didn't care. All she cared about were the people who were meant to be under her protection. "Tell me what I have to do to secure the release of my men, or I will walk away."

"Your men are already being released," the Master of Crows said. "I do not need their deaths, when you will provide so many more."

"I've just told you that I won't do what you want," Sophia said. She meant it. That this thing wanted her to invade the Dowager's kingdom was only one more reason not to do it.

The Master of Crows shrugged. "In battle, a commander's intentions do not matter if they cannot see the whole situation. They find themselves reacting as it changes, and he who controls those changes can make them dance like puppets."

"Is that why you go to war?" Sophia asked. "To watch people perform for you?"

"There is a certain joy in it," the Master of Crows admitted, sounding pleased by it. "But mostly I do it because I realized the truth a long time ago."

"What truth?" Sophia asked.

The New Army's leader smiled. "That if it comes to a choice between my life and the world, I will see the world in ashes. My creatures must be fed to sustain me. They *will* be fed. There is little point in fighting against it."

Sophia shook her head. "You're trying to make it sound as if it's inevitable. As if it's my destiny. Well, I still get to choose, and I'm choosing to walk up that beach and go back to the castle. Try to stop me, and I'll have Sienne rip out your throat."

"You think I am without protection?" the Master of Crows asked, with a gesture to his still circling birds.

"I think that cats *eat* birds," Sophia pointed out. She turned to leave.

To her surprise, she heard the Master of Crows laughing behind her. Sophia spun back toward him.

"What's so funny?"

"Simply that you truly believe you will do this thing, when I can stop you with a word. With four words, to be more precise."

Did he mean some spell, or some trick? Should Sophia be trying to protect herself?

"Are you ready?" the Master of Crows asked. He held up one gloved hand, ready to count off the words as he said them. "Would you like to hear my four words? Here they are: Sebastian is in danger."

Sophia froze, unable to help herself. Sebastian couldn't be in danger, could he? This man, this *thing,* was lying to her. Even so, she couldn't bring herself to walk away.

"Would you like to see?" The Master of Crows held out a hand like a falconer, and a bird plunged down from the circling mass to land on it. This one was larger than the others, a raven rather than a crow, and it stared at Sophia with the same bleak black eyes as its owner. Sienne hissed at it as it landed. The Master of Crows held it out to her, and Sophia realized that he was expecting her to hold her own arm out to take it.

Sophia felt certain that this had to be some kind of trick, but she didn't dare to walk away. If Sebastian was truly in danger, and she ignored it, then she would feel as guilty as if she'd hurt him herself. Hesitantly, not knowing if it was the right thing, Sophia lifted her arm. The bird was heavier than Sophia had thought it might be, weighing down her arm as it hopped across. It dug in with its claws, and Sophia saw...

She watched from a bird's-eye view as Sebastian stood at docks she recognized as Ashton's. She saw men surrounding him, grabbing him, dragging him away. She saw a figure she recognized as Rupert...

"When was this?" Sophia demanded. "What am I seeing?"

"Watch," the Master of Crows said, with a smile that said he knew he had her now, and that she wouldn't be able to look away.

Sebastian being bundled into a cart, driven through the streets of the city to a house that was large and forbidding from the outside. Being dragged inside. The bird moving lower, prompted by an unseen hand, looking through the windows of a basement kitchen so that it could see Sebastian being dragged through it toward a basement door...

"There were no windows beyond that," the Master of Crows said. "No way for one of my pets to get close. But I think it's enough to show you what is happening. I have heard more, of course. They forget to shoot at crows there. Prince Sebastian walked out of his wedding, then disappeared. The Dowager is most angry with Prince Rupert, and tried to send him away, although my pets say that he has not gone. Sebastian languishes in Rupert's home. Tell me, what do you think is happening to him there?"

"Rupert wouldn't hurt Sebastian," Sophia said, but the truth was that she could imagine the possibilities all too easily. She knew what Rupert was capable of. She'd seen it firsthand, when he'd tried to force himself on her. "Or maybe this isn't real. Maybe you're lying to me."

"If you truly believe that," the Master of Crows said. "Simply do nothing. I don't think you will."

Sophia glared at him. She hated being manipulated like this, made to dance in his game, yet the truth was that she didn't have a choice.

"I will withdraw to my ships," the Master of Crows said. "Ishjemme will not be attacked, for now. Instead, I will wait for the outcome of your war with the Dowager."

"And attack whoever is weakened by it," Sophia guessed.

The Master of Crows didn't even try to deny it. "Crows follow in the aftermath of battle."

"We'll be ready for you," Sophia promised. She reached out to hand the tall man his raven back, but the creature dug into her arm, snapping at her with its beak. Sophia jerked back only just in time to keep from losing an ear to the thing, shaking it loose from her arm and striking at it. It hopped from her to the Master of Crows, settling on his shoulder easily.

"It seems that my pets will not be satisfied without at least a taste of you," he said. He turned to the creature, and it seemed for a moment as if he were listening to it. "An ear. They will have one lovely ear, as a promise of things to come."

Sophia stepped back, behind the strength of Sienne. The forest cat was crouched now, ready to spring.

"Stay away from me," Sophia commanded. "I'm not going to let your creatures near me. I'm certainly not going to let that thing eat my ear."

The Master of Crows laughed at that. He drew a slender blade, holding it with the kind of ease that came from long practice.

"Oh, you still don't understand how this all works, do you? You still think that you're in control. You still think that you get to *let* me do anything."

Sophia drew her eating knife. It seemed so pitiful against the blade her opponent held, yet, as he advanced, the circling cloud of sand keeping all help out, it was all Sophia had.

CHAPTER SEVENTEEN

Lucas stood watching the wall of dust stirred up by the crows with disquiet, even though he knew the swirl of it probably protected their people from the New Army's ships as much as it hid all that was going on within it. He felt a touch of relief as men came in from the shore, stumbling out of the dust in the colors of Ishjemme.

Even so, he stood as taut as a drawn bowstring, a hand on his sword ready to draw it. He didn't trust this. He could feel the power of the creature who had come to them, and he didn't like leaving his sister alone with him, with *it*.

He felt the moment when his sister was in danger like a blade sliding into his flesh. He heard her cry out for help in his mind as clearly as if she were standing next to him shouting.

Help!

Lucas didn't hesitate, didn't look around for the others or try to ask what was happening. Instead, he sprang forward on instinct, running forward, plunging into the cloud of dust and sand as he sought to get to Sophia in time.

I'm coming, Sophia, he sent, but there was no time for more than that. He was too busy fighting his way through the dust.

It *was* a fight. The sand and dust that the Master of Crows' magic had stirred up stung Lucas's flesh as he pressed forward, scouring him with the feel of wire wool running over a sword. It got in his eyes, so that Lucas had to screw them tight against the blinding grit of it. It seemed almost like a living thing trying to push him back, or make him lost so that he would never find his sister.

Lucas didn't need to be able to see to find Sophia though. He could feel her presence ahead as surely as he knew where his limbs were, or which way was up. Where someone else might have staggered through the dust cloud a pace at a time, Lucas ran, trusting that if he got to Sophia, nothing else mattered.

Help, she called again. Lucas drew his sword, ready to strike down anything that threatened her.

He came out into a clear space at the heart of the dust storm, where Sophia stood, backing away from the Master of Crows as the man advanced on her with a blade in his hand.

"You're being unreasonable about this," he said. "It is only an ear that my pets want for now. I will have it, so why not be still?"

"Leave her alone!" Lucas shouted, and the other man turned to face him, looking at Lucas as if trying to work out exactly what he was.

"Hmm, maybe you'll do even better than an ear," he said.

He opened his coat and birds flew out. They poured from it, they sped from it. They came straight for Lucas's face, and he barely ducked in time. Even so, claws scratched at his shoulders, beaks pecked at his skin. Lucas forced himself not to panic. Official Ko had once had him recite poetry while servants threw feathers and rice sacks at him, rats and small snakes. Compared with that, Lucas could deal with a storm of crows.

Hacking left and right with his sword, he started to cut his way through it. He found a feline shape accompanying him, Sophia's forest cat bringing down birds with great swipes of her claws.

A blade appeared through the chaos, and Lucas barely parried it in time. The birds flew back, leaving him facing the Master of Crows while Sienne moved to Sophia's side, obviously determined to protect her. Lucas's blade didn't waver as he leveled it at his foe's heart.

"You should let me kill you now," the Master of Crows said. "I have never been bested with a blade, and it will be quicker for you that way. Aren't you afraid of the pain I could inflict on you? The way I'll make you scream for death?"

Lucas smiled. "I had many sword masters," he said. "One of them once told me that the threats a man makes when he fights mean nothing for you. They only tell you the things that those men fear."

The Master of Crows roared his anger at that, and grabbed for a pistol at his belt so fast that most people wouldn't have been able to react. Lucas was already diving out of the way, though, as the shot went past. He rolled, coming up to his feet in time to parry a series of thrusts.

His opponent was skilled; there was no doubt of that. He thrust and cut relentlessly, but without leaving obvious openings, his attacks were forceful without being clumsy, sophisticated without being needlessly complex, ruthless and direct at the same time. Lucas gave ground to a lunge, then had to parry quickly as his opponent followed it up with a dropping attack aimed at his legs. He felt sure that the least mistake would mean death against a foe like this.

Even so, Lucas started to counterattack. He cut at the Master of Crows' arm as he came in, then beat his blade aside, slicing so close to him that it cut through the lining of his coat. His opponent barely missed him with a sweeping cut aimed at Lucas's head, but Lucas swayed aside in time. He had more sense than to try to take the obvious opening that created, because the Master of Crows' blade was already cutting down to cover it.

"You have some skill," the other man acknowledged. "Let's see how much."

He came forward with a blistering series of attacks, at a speed most people would barely have seen. Lucas's blade wove patterns in the air as he deflected blow after blow, batting them aside or just blocking them outright. It was hard, his own reflexes pushed hard by the powers his blood gave to him. He caught the Master of Crows' blade for a moment on his guard, then cut down, slicing into him from shoulder to chest.

Against anyone else it would have been a fatal blow. With this opponent, though, it meant that Lucas had to grab hurriedly for the other man's sword arm as his blade found itself briefly stuck.

"No one has wounded me like that in a long time," the Master of Crows said, pushing close to Lucas.

"I'll do more than wound you," Lucas promised.

"My crows give me life, boy. As long as I feed them death, you cannot beat me."

He had a knife in his other hand now, and Lucas could see the dilemma: if he let go of the other man's sword arm to deal with it, he would be vulnerable. If he didn't...

A shape slammed into the Master of Crows from the side, knocking him back. Lucas saw Sienne snapping and snarling at him, leaping back as the New Army's general swiped at her. It was enough to buy him time, and Lucas used the moment to wrench his sword clear.

"I doubt even your crows can save you if I cut your head off," he said, raising his blade again.

The Master of Crows stood there, obviously trying to weigh his chances of winning the fight hampered with a wound; Lucas suspected that he was trying to work out exactly how much an ear was worth to him.

Apparently not his life. He sprang back into the dust and the sand swirling around him. A part of Lucas wanted to give chase and hunt him through that dust by just the traces of his mind. That would be a dangerous game though. It was better to wait for a better chance. His sister needed him.

He turned to Sophia then, looking her over, trying to make sure she wasn't wounded.

"Are you all right?" he asked.

She nodded. "Are *you*? The way you fought then... it reminded me of the way Kate fights. It was incredible."

"I had good teachers," Lucas said, cleaning his sword and sheathing it.

"He wanted to take my ear," Sophia said. "He's... he's something not human. All he cares about is creating chaos to feed those crows of his."

Lucas shuddered at that thought, and at how powerful it might make someone.

"Why did he come here?" Lucas asked. "What did he want?"

"He told me something," Sophia said. "Something that... it will mean more war, more violence."

"More food for his crows," Lucas guessed.

He saw Sophia bite her lip. "Yes, but I can't ignore it. What he said... I can't leave things as they are."

Lucas reached out to put a hand on his sister's shoulder. "Whatever you decide, I will be there."

She hugged him then, holding him tight. "You don't know how glad I am that you found us."

Lucas had an idea, because he knew just how grateful he was that he'd found his sister. When he pulled back from the hug, he turned slowly, looking for signs of the Master of Crows' pets, but they seemed to be gone now, fled along with their master. Around them, the dust was already starting to settle, falling in gentle waves as the wind caught it, thinning so that it was possible to see shadows through it, then clearing completely.

He found the others waiting on the banks of the fjord, their captured men standing free beside them. The surprising part came when he looked out over the water. The ships that had been there were gone, already disappeared around the bends of the waterway.

"Where did they go?" Sophia asked. "How did they get away so quickly?"

"They must have already been moving while we were in the dust," Lucas said.

Their uncle came over to them, wrapping strong arms around them both. "I'm so glad you're safe," he said. "When you were both in there with that man, when the ships turned to go... I was sure he must have killed you or captured you."

Lucas shook his head. "He would need to be a much better swordsman to do that."

He thought then of all the training that Official Ko had put him through, all the hours that he had spent with tutors. Everyone had said that they were training him to rule, but maybe the old man had been more cunning than that. Lucas had certainly never managed to plumb the depths of his long thought out ideas. Maybe he'd guessed that Lucas would want no part of being a king if it meant pushing his sister aside. Maybe he'd trained him to be all he needed to be to protect her instead.

The sheer enormity of that hit him then, with all that it might mean. The idea that all of this might have been planned, by their parents, by the creatures that sought to rule, by beings with the knowledge to make choices that would change the world. There wasn't any time to think about it, though, because Sophia was already speaking, addressing her cousins, her uncle, and the men gathered there.

"The Master of Crows came here today to try to manipulate me," Sophia said. "He wanted to force me into war. I will not go into war because he makes me, but I *will* go to war. The Dowager has taken someone I love. Her kingdom oppresses those who are like me, like *us*. It is clear that attacks will come, if not now, then soon. Will you fight alongside me?"

They cheered, and Lucas surprised himself by cheering with them. Every word of it only confirmed to Lucas that he'd done the right thing stepping aside. Sophia was the one who could make people follow her. She was the one who could cut through the moves and countermoves, to the things that mattered. She was the one with the skills to lead, and Lucas would protect her while she did it, from the Master of Crows, or anything else.

"Uncle, cousins," she said. "I want you to prepare whatever armies Ishjemme can muster. I want you to send messages to our allies, so that armies come down from the mountain clans and rise up among the lords. We're going to Ashton, and we're going to retake my kingdom."

CHAPTER EIGHTEEN

Angelica waited until Rupert was out about some business in the city before she headed down to the cellars and the hidden door that sat there. Rupert probably thought that she didn't know about any of his secrets yet, but Angelica had always been quick when it came to finding what was hidden, and there was hardly a member of the household who didn't know the rumors of what Rupert did down here.

The screams of the servant who had betrayed him had given quite a lot of it away.

She moved carefully. She was working to secure the loyalty of some of the staff there, had brought in some of her own people, but she didn't have all of them so quickly, and it would only take one reporting this to Rupert. She had the bruises on her to declare exactly how dangerously unpredictable he could be. She moved by the light of a hooded lantern, sliding back the barrels as quietly as she could, then creeping into the space beyond.

Sebastian's cell was the only occupied one. It made things simpler in its way, meaning that she didn't have to kill any of the other prisoners to keep them quiet. The sight of him there, blinking at her in the lamplight, should probably have brought pity. Instead, she felt anger rising in her, cold and hard as steel.

"Angelica?" he said, in a hopeful tone, as if she were his salvation. "What are you doing down here?"

"You mean, am I here to get you out?" Angelica asked. "Why should I, Sebastian? Why should I, after *all you've done*?"

She let him have a glimpse of her hurt then. Of her hurt, and of the anger that it had turned into. Rupert might have done this to his brother, but this, *this* was her revenge.

"Angelica," Sebastian said, "I'm sorry, I know I've hurt you, but—"

"But you did it because you love that whore Sophia, so that's all right," Angelica finished for him. She didn't bother trying to hide her contempt for what he'd done. "You think that because you're doing it for love, you can hurt who you like. Do you know that your mother tried to have me killed?"

Sebastian looked at her in shock. "She wouldn't…"

"Don't be a fool," Angelica snapped back. She didn't want to hear his well-meaning blindness to the evil in others' hearts. "Those in power get there by being the strongest, the cruelest, or the most cunning. You know perfectly well how many people the Dowager has killed over the years. She was going to add me to the list for failing to seduce you well enough. For failing to get you into the kind of marriage that a proper prince should have."

"Angelica, I didn't know," Sebastian said. Angelica guessed that was probably the truth. It didn't make a difference. At best, it said that Sebastian was thoughtless and stupid. But no matter how much Angelica tried to tell herself that, she still had trouble thinking about anything but him.

"You didn't know that you were doing harm when you walked out on me?" she demanded. "You didn't know that you were running to the daughter of your mother's old enemies? You thought that it was all right to leave me, not once, but twice?"

Sebastian nodded. "You're right," he said, "I've done a lot to hurt you, but we could make it right. You could still get me out of here, and then we could go across the sea, where my mother wouldn't be able to touch you. We could go to Ishjemme together."

"Where I would get to watch you marry *her*?" Angelica demanded. Was Sebastian really stupid enough to think that she would do something that would rob her of everything she'd worked for? Did he think that she was so blindly in love with him that she would give up everything the way…

…the way he had for Sophia? That thought just made Angelica angrier.

"I'm not going to run off on some fool's errand with you," she said. "I'm not going to give up everything for a man who isn't ruthless enough to take the throne."

"Is that all you care about?" Sebastian demanded. He grabbed the bars of his prison. "I thought I saw another side to you, Angelica. I thought you were a better person than that. I thought you *cared*."

On impulse, Angelica grabbed him, kissing him through the bars, quick and deep, pulling Sebastian to her so that she could taste his mouth on hers, feel him close enough that he was almost a part of her. She did it because she wanted to, because she could, and yes, maybe because she did feel something for her lovely prince. Those feelings just made what he'd done hurt more, so she shoved him back, stepping away from the bars.

"You talk about caring as if it matters," Angelica said as she wiped the taste of him from her mouth. "It doesn't change anything in the world. It doesn't protect you from the people who want to hurt you. It doesn't give you power, or strength, or safety. It doesn't make it hurt less when people *betray* you."

That was the point Angelica needed to hang onto here. She was the wronged party in this. She was the one who had been put aside and attacked, pushed into a situation where there were almost no choices. She would not apologize for doing what was necessary to live.

She would not forgive Sebastian. But she would use him.

"You're going to rot here," she said. "You humiliated me, and I will not forgive that. I'm not going to throw away everything to free you."

"Angelica," Sebastian said. "Rupert is planning to install himself as the heir!"

He said it as if it were a warning. As if he were somehow saving her from some terrible fate. Maybe he was relying on her doing the right thing. Whatever his reason, Angelica laughed at it.

"Why do you think I'm marrying him?" she replied.

It was worth it just to see the hurt on Sebastian's face. It went a little way toward repaying the hurt he'd visited on her. Not far enough though. Not by a long way.

"You're marrying Rupert?" Sebastian said, and he had the temerity to sound as though he were the one who had been betrayed. He made it sound as though, having been put aside by him, Angelica should have retired quietly from public life.

"What did you think would happen?" Angelica demanded. "We could have married. We could have been king and queen of this island in time. I would have helped you to be great, although the Masked Goddess knows I'd have spent half the time trying to make up for your naiveté."

"It's not naïve to want to do the right thing," Sebastian said.

If the bars hadn't been in the way, Angelica might have slapped him then, just to try to break through his stupidity. There were some people who couldn't be woken up to the world, though.

"And who do you think manages to do the most good in the world?" Angelica demanded. "The fool who gives up his path to the crown, or the one who takes that crown by force and then uses it to make a safe, prosperous kingdom?"

"Things won't be either of those with Rupert in charge," Sebastian said. "You know what he's like, Angelica."

She did, probably better than Sebastian did. She was *counting* on it. Rupert was her way to move from merely being a member of a respected noble family to having real power. He was the sword that would cut an opening for her to step through.

"You could let me out," Sebastian said. "You could find a way to do it without Rupert learning it was you, I'm sure of it. You could still… if you really want to do it, you could still marry him."

"Thank you for being so gracious as to tell me who I can marry," Angelica said in a cold tone. Who did Sebastian think he was, to ask her to take that risk? Who did he think he was, giving her *permission* to marry Rupert?

"Do you know what's going to happen to you, Sebastian?" she said. "You're going to stay right here. You're going to stay here, and you're going to rot. You're right, I probably could let you out now, but I don't want to. I have no reason to. You're going to disappear from the world, locked in the dark. It's going to be your punishment for everything you've done to me."

"Then why are you even here?" Sebastian asked.

He really was a fool, Angelica decided. A beautiful one, but a fool nonetheless.

"Because I can be," she said. "Because I want to hurt you. Because I want to make the point that you're in my power, as much as Rupert's. I'm going to marry him, and you're going to spend your life wondering what might have happened if only you'd gone through with it instead of running off."

She watched his face, seeking out the hurt there. She wanted this to hurt. He deserved for it to hurt.

"I'm going to become Rupert's queen when he rules," she said. "And that will be soon enough. Your mother will pay for trying to kill me."

"A lot of people have gone up against her before," Sebastian said.

"And they died for it because they weren't ruthless enough, or they didn't hold the right cards," Angelica said. "Well, I hold both of her sons. I'll have Rupert for a husband soon enough, and you…"

Maybe she shouldn't say it, but she did anyway.

"Maybe I won't keep you locked away in here all the time," she said. "Maybe I'll have you brought out when I want you, cleaned up and brought to my bedroom. The nobles of this kingdom treat girls like me as if we're brood mares, so maybe I should treat you that way."

"I—" Sebastian began.

95

"You wouldn't have a choice!" Angelica snapped at him. "You could have been my partner, but now, I will decide what you are, and if it's my plaything, then that's what you will end up being!"

She could see the look of disgust on Sebastian's face, and that just made her angrier. How dare he feel such a thing toward her?

"Do you think Rupert would stand for that?" he asked.

"Rupert will never know," Angelica said. "It's not as if he's any brighter than you are. Maybe I should have gone after him from the start of this, but I had the foolish idea that you were the better man. I've been cured of that delusion, at least."

She turned to go, then turned back to him, wanting to see him there, helpless; wanting to hurt him in one more way.

"Don't think I've forgotten about Sophia, either," she said. "She's been behind too much of this, and she's still an impediment, given her claim to the throne. I do not allow obstacles to stay in my path, and I do not forgive an insult."

"If you hurt her…" Sebastian began.

"What will you do?" Angelica asked. "You're stuck in a cell, with no way to so much as get a message out. I, on the other hand, can send messages to the kinds of people who will see your whore dead. I already have."

There was even more satisfaction than she'd thought in seeing Sebastian trying to wrench his way through the bars. Angelica liked seeing that futile anger, because it said that she'd managed to hurt him the way he deserved to be hurt.

"You should have listened to me, Sebastian," she said as she turned to walk away again. "You should have married me. We could have ruled together. Now, you're going to stay here, and your precious Sophia is going to die."

She walked away, picturing Sebastian watching her as she left. He was primed now. When she decided to act, he would do all that she wanted him to do.

CHAPTER NINETEEN

Kate couldn't remember a time when she hadn't been in pain. Agony stretched into the past, filling so much of it that she couldn't look past it. She couldn't remember how long she'd been there, couldn't work out if it had been minutes, hours, days, or years. All she could remember was the pain of a hundred or more different torments.

She burst free of the grip of a masked nun, then ran down a corridor filled with flailing arms, each ending in a clawed hand. The claws slashed at her, burning as they cut through her flesh, making her scream as she pressed forward. The wounds healed instantly, because there was no flesh to wound here, but that didn't stop the pain.

"Please," she begged, in spite of herself, "make it stop."

She had once thought that she was the kind of person who would never beg anyone for anything. She hadn't been afraid of whatever pain Siobhan could inflict on her; she'd only done what the woman of the fountain wanted when she threatened Sophia. She hadn't buckled under the efforts of the masked nuns, or the violence of Ashton's streets. Kate had thought she was strong enough to withstand anything the world could throw at her.

This wasn't in the world, though, and it was breaking her, piece by piece.

Kate ran on, and now she was moving through a swampy landscape where the air was foul enough to burn her lungs, and flares of gas caught fire, singeing her as she passed. There were creatures there that struck at her: snakes and lizards, scaled things that tried to pierce her flesh with fangs or strike at her with claws.

The worst part of it was that there seemed to be no end to it. Kate couldn't see the glimmering silver thread of the path; hadn't been able to in so long that it seemed almost like her imagination. This wasn't like some torture in the world, where she could have stopped it simply by giving someone what they wanted. This was a place where there was nothing she could do to end the agony, the constant violence and the fear.

She wondered what would happen when she finally ran out of the will to resist, or ran out of hope, or just gave in. Would what was left of her be torn to shreds? Would she merge into this hellish landscape? Or would it just go on without cease until the end of time, while out in the world Siobhan rode her body in an attempt to kill Sophia?

"No," Kate swore. "I won't allow it. I'll find a way to stop it."

That need, that connection, drove her on. If this were just about her pain, maybe she would have sunk into it, maybe she would have even deserved it, but she couldn't let Siobhan kill Sophia. She couldn't let the witch do what she'd threatened, and take over the body of Kate's unborn niece. Kate would press on until she found a way to stop that, whatever it cost her.

She felt something then, in a ripple that seemed to move through this space beyond the physical world. There was something familiar about it; something that felt almost the way it felt when she connected with Sophia's mind, yet it *wasn't* her mind. There was something different about this. It felt... almost like a boy's mind?

Kate frowned at that, and a part of her thought it must be some kind of trick. It had to be a trap, because *everything* here was a trap. Every scrap of hope here was just to draw her into more pain, every hint of respite only there to make the pain that followed worse.

She had to risk it though. If there was a chance that it might let her help Sophia, she had to grab hold of it. Kate stood still for a moment, ignoring the things that raked at her skin, trying to give a direction to what she felt even though this was a place where normal directions didn't apply. Kate fixed it in her mind, turned...

...and ran.

She sprinted, ignoring everything in between, her feet carrying her across space that wasn't space, moving her to a point where it felt as though the air became thicker. Kate pushed through it, forcing her way forward through something that felt like a curtain.

Then it was a curtain, or at least a screen made from silk. Kate brushed it aside with her hand like cobwebs, and found herself in a room with wooden floors, covered in the most elaborately woven rugs she'd ever seen. There were paintings on the walls that seemed to strive to convey the essence of their subjects in as few lines as possible. Looking through a window, she could see gardens that rose in a well-fed green space, despite the appearance of sandy dunes in the distance.

Was this some new place for her to suffer, or was it something else?

She could hear voices beyond the room, and Kate crept forward cautiously to the doorway. Beyond, she could see a fat man with a sallow complexion wrapped in silken robes, seated on something close to a throne. Her attention was on the two figures in front of him, though, because she knew them. She'd seen them in her dreams and in her memories.

What were her parents doing here?

"Will he be safe here, Ko?" her mother asked.

The fat man put a hand over his heart. "You know that I will defend him with my life, Christina. Do you have any doubts?"

"No, old friend," Kate's father said. "There is no one else we could have brought him to. We just fear the Dowager's power."

"*That* is not something that can touch the Silk Lands," the fat man said.

"There are other powers in the world that can," Kate's mother pointed out.

The fat man bowed his head. "That is true, but you have done all that you can. Now, would you like to go and say farewell to… what is the child's name?"

"Lucas," Kate's mother said. "His name is Lucas."

They left, and the fat man sat there alone for a while. He looked over to the doorway.

"You can come out," he said.

Kate walked forward, uncertain if she should, not knowing if this was just a prelude to some new kind of torture.

"What is all this?" she asked. "Who are you?"

"I believe the custom is that the guest goes first," the fat man said.

"I'm Kate," she said, still looking around. The room was simple in so many ways, but where there were carvings or tapestries, they were of a quality that would have put most palaces to shame. "Those… they're my parents, or they were, or… what is this place?"

"A dream, a memory, something else," the fat man said. "I am Official Ko. Well no, that isn't true. The real me is in the world somewhere. I am a fragment given more life than it should have, nothing more. And you have the look of someone who is hunted."

Kate nodded. She imagined that even now, the things that had been torturing her would be trying to find her. She half expected the man in front of her to turn into one of them at any moment.

"Are you one of them?" she asked.

The fat man shook his head. "I am not. I would say that you are safe here, but I suspect that isn't true, not forever. There is only so long that a good dream can keep the bad ones at bay. We only have so much time, and I imagine that there are questions you want to ask."

There was one that came to Kate immediately. "Where are my parents?"

Official Ko shook his head. "I am just a faded old memory. I do not know what passes in the world. Try again."

Kate frowned trying to think. "Who is Lucas?"

Official Ko stood, gesturing to the door. "That, we can answer. Come."

Kate followed the man, or the memory of a man, or whatever he was, heading through the door into a corridor that seemed to stretch forever.

"How does this place exist?" she asked. "How are you here?"

"It is hard to say," Official Ko said. "Your family is special, and I taught Lucas many things. This place was originally a place in which to store memories so that they would not be forgotten. A way to learn. Your presence probably makes this place more than it was."

Kate looked into one of the rooms. She could see a young boy there, working to write on a clay tablet, his tongue poking out of the corner of his mouth as he concentrated.

"You understand who he is, don't you?" the fat man asked.

"He's my brother," Kate said, and just saying the words felt like a realization. "I have... I have a brother."

It felt right somehow. It felt *true.* Kate didn't know how she knew it, but she could feel the reality of it. She had a brother. She wanted to shout it to the world. She stared at him then, not wanting to take her eyes off this boy, wanting to know all about the brother she'd never known she had.

"There are more doorways," Official Ko said.

Kate followed him to the cusp of each one, and behind each, it seemed that there was another scene from her brother's life. There he was, playing a hiding game with a collection of servants. There he was, reciting passages from a book that Kate had never heard of. She saw him practicing with weapons, plotting out tactics with wooden soldiers, learning to play instruments that looked like nothing Kate had seen before. Each moment that she saw felt precious, both because it let her see something of her brother's life, and because it was a moment in which she wasn't suffering at the hands of whatever lay beyond this place's walls.

Then those walls started to crack, and claws began to reach through.

"Ah, I feared this might happen," the image of Official Ko said. "This is a haven, but it is not a fortress, and in this place, creatures seek life, and light, and pain."

"What can I do?" Kate asked.

There were two swords in the fat man's hands now, both curved and long. He passed one to Kate.

"You can go," he said, gesturing to the doorways. "Do what you know you must. I… well, I am just an old image, but I will hold them as long as I can."

"Thank you," Kate said.

Official Ko smiled. "Thank your brother. I think he remembers this version of me better than I am." He pointed. "That door, I think."

The first of the creatures broke through, and Official Ko raised his sword. Kate wished that she could stay and fight, but instead, she ran through the door the image had pointed to. She found herself in a walled courtyard, where a young man with flame red hair was practicing with a blade of his own. He turned to Kate as she approached, and even though she knew this wasn't the real Lucas, it felt as though she was meeting her brother for the first time in that moment. She could feel the pulse of connection to him, and she just hoped that it would be enough.

"Who are you?" he asked. "What are you doing here?"

"There's no time," she said, then sent the words as forcefully as she could.

If you can hear me, I'm trapped. Our sister is in danger. A witch has taken my form. You must save her. You must save us both.

It was all that there was time for. The creatures were already pouring into the courtyard, and this time, Kate suspected that they weren't going to give her another chance to run to safety.

She lifted her blade, and charged.

CHAPTER TWENTY

Sophia watched her people preparing for war, and she was proud of them even as she feared what might happen to them in what was to come. She put one hand over her belly protectively as she watched them loading ships and sharpening weapons. The other went to ruffle Sienne's fur. Was she really going to bring her child into a world at war, or risk its well-being in the violence that would follow? Was she really going to risk all the people who were gathering and training together, readying themselves for the war to come?

With Sebastian in danger, she would. To give her child back its father, to rescue the man she loved, she would burn the world if she had to.

"You're worried about what's coming," Lucas said, standing beside her at the docks. He looked ready for war in a way that Sophia didn't feel. He'd probably been preparing for it over the years where all Sophia had learned was to fear the masked nuns who tormented her.

"I'm terrified by it," she admitted. "Am I doing the right thing, Lucas? You know more about war than I do, I think. Is this attack the right thing to do?"

You shouldn't second-guess yourself aloud, Lucas sent over to her. *People need to see that you're confident. They draw their strength from you. They trust you.*

Sophia had been surprised to find that it was true, but it seemed to be. The men there watched her as she passed, bowing low or calling out their support. The captains of their forces came up to her as she and Lucas started to tour the preparations, and it seemed that every one of them had a report or a question.

"Will we assault Ashton along its river?" one man asked. "My men are skilled in beaching boats in shallow water."

Sophia looked over to Lucas.

It is a valid tactic, he sent. *It might let us get men inside the city. It depends how quickly they could move up the river.*

That was one thing where Sophia felt that she knew enough to comment. She'd seen the river that ran through Ashton. She knew how many barges were there. Her friend Emeline had told her the stories of piloting one. Just imagining it, she knew the answer.

"We couldn't do it openly," she said. "If they saw us coming, there are enough boats on the river that they could blockade it. They can close off the bridges or raise chains. If they judge it right, they could trap us."

The captain looked disappointed at his idea being rejected like that, but Sophia wasn't done.

"But that's if we do it openly," she said. "So what I want you to do is find trading vessels, and get your men aboard wearing none of Ishjemme's colors. Get them to Ashton, and when the time comes, I want you to be in a position to take the river for us to give us access. Can you do that?"

The man nodded. "Yes, my queen."

My queen. It was still strange being called that. Strange having men who probably knew more about war than Sophia did looking to her for answers.

You're doing better than I could, Lucas sent to her. *I can tell a man the tactics Official Ko had me learn, but I do not know the Dowager's kingdom, and I cannot make the men here love me as they love you.*

Sophia wasn't so sure about that. The men nodded to Lucas as he passed. She could sense the respect there for a warrior more skilled than almost any of them. Sophia had seen what he could do when he fought the Master of Crows. She had no doubt that the men would follow him when it came to battle.

"Things seem to be going well," she said, although even to her it sounded more like a question than a statement. It was hard to tell, when there was so much happening on the docks. Was this what things looked like when they were going well, or was this the kind of chaos that could lead to disaster?

"They're going well," Lucas assured her. He nodded to where their cousins were working hard to coordinate things. "Hans has the men drilling ready for battle, while Oli is keeping notes of the supplies as they go aboard. Freya and Ulf are helping with the merchants, Jan is captaining a ship, and Endi is gathering messages as they come in."

Sophia smiled at how quickly her brother was managing to keep track of things.

I was serious about helping and advising you, he sent. *A queen doesn't have to do everything herself. You get help, and you have all the family to help anyone could wish for.*

Not all *the family,* Sophia sent back. *We still have to find our parents.*

"We will," Lucas assured her aloud. "But first, we will do this."

Sophia nodded, then turned to the castle. "We should head back for now. It will still be a little while before we're ready to go, and our uncle will want to be updated about what's happening."

"And you should rest a little," Lucas said. "I know you're strong, but this is a lot when you are pregnant."

Sophia nodded. She *was* tired. Just walking to tour the preparations for the invasion was hard work, but she wasn't going to complain about it when everyone else was doing so much.

They walked back in the direction of the castle, passing people in the streets as they went. Some bowed or curtseyed, and that felt a little stranger than with the soldiers, especially when so many of them were going on with their normal lives while around them, preparations for war were still taking place. Sophia could see a washer woman hanging out clothes while almost next to her a man sorted through musket balls for any that were too flat, or too rough. She walked past a bakery where people were laughing with one another, but a glance at their thoughts showed that they were thinking about the sons who were going off to Ashton, possibly never to come back.

The closer they got to the castle, though, the more people were focused on war. There were more soldiers there, and fewer ordinary people. As Sophia, Sienne, and Lucas approached, two of the soldiers came up to them, and Sophia could see in their thoughts what had them moving with that much urgency.

"Kate's back?" she asked.

One nodded. "Yes, your majesty. Your sister arrived just a little while ago. She said she needed to see you as soon as you came back."

"Where is she?" Sophia asked.

"She is waiting for you in your chambers."

Sophia nodded. "Thank you. Will you take Sienne? She needs to be fed, and I doubt I'll have a chance now."

"Yes, my queen." The guard sounded hesitant. Was it that they were still nervous around the forest cat, or were they worried about her being without protection? Either way, there was no reason to worry. Sienne did as Sophia asked, while Sophia doubted that she would need the forest cat's extra protection for a family reunion.

Go with them, Sophia sent to Sienne, *they'll find you food.*

The forest cat briefly pushed against Sophia's leg, but then went, following one of the guards. Sophia and Lucas went in together, making their way through the castle. Around them, things were as busy as everywhere else in Ishjemme, with people running about in their preparations. The whole place felt almost like a crossbow being wound back, ready to launch the bolt of its invasion fleet.

But before that, Sophia needed to let her sister know that they had a brother.

She and Lucas went up through the castle toward the rooms that were Sophia's now. There were no guards by the doors, but only because Sophia would have felt uncomfortable sleeping in any room that needed guards. She opened the doors, stepping inside with Lucas.

"There you are," she said as she saw her sister standing by one of the windows. She ran up to Kate to hug her. "I've been so worried about you!"

"I'm fine," Kate assured her. She seemed a little uncomfortable being hugged like that and quickly turned her attention to Lucas. "Who is this? Can we send him away? We need to talk."

That seemed blunt, even by Kate's standards.

Is something wrong? Sophia sent across to her, but Kate had walls up across her mind in a way that she never normally did around her. Something must be really wrong if Kate didn't even want Sophia to see it like that, but the sheer magnitude of the good news that she had outweighed the rest of it.

"Kate, this is Lucas. He... he's our brother."

"Our brother?" Kate stared at him, and Sophia could see the surprise there now. "We have a brother?"

"We do," Sophia said. "Our parents hid him and..." A thought occurred to her. "Our parents. Now that Kate is here, we can find them with your device, Lucas."

"What device?" Kate asked.

Sophia did her best to explain. "Lucas came because of our messages to the Silk Lands. Our parents aren't there, but they left him with a device that would find them if the three of us were brought together. We can find them, Kate."

Her sister cocked her head to the side. "Let's not get ahead of ourselves."

That caught Sophia a little by surprise. "Kate, you've wanted to find our parents even more than I have," she said. "This is our chance. What's happened to you?"

Kate seemed to think for a few moments, looking from Sophia to Lucas and back. "I went to try to break my link to Siobhan," she explained, and Sophia gaped at her.

"How could you do something that dangerous without telling me?" she asked. "Kate, that must have been so dangerous!"

"It was," Kate said. "The witch who helped me, Haxa, is dead. It was… a difficult experience for me, too. I think it might have changed some things about me. I'm not the person I was. It's why I don't know if this device is a good idea. I don't even know if it will work for me."

"It should work for us," Lucas said. "It is in our blood."

Kate paused. "Well," she allowed, "I guess I still have the same blood."

Lucas took out the flat disc of metal that he had shown to Sophia before. As it had then, it glowed faintly where he touched it, letters and lines gleaming in response to his power.

Sophia reached out, touching it too, and the interlocking pieces of the device started to shift, moving around to form the map of the world that they had before. Its lines glowed, and Sophia wanted to believe that when Kate touched it, the spot where her parents stood would be revealed.

"Now you," Sophia said to Kate.

Lucas frowned as she spoke, looking almost as if he were listening to something Sophia couldn't hear. Sophia focused on Kate, though, because this was a moment that they had all hoped for. This was the moment when they would finally find their parents. Kate reached out for the disc of metal, touching it delicately…

Lucas's eyes widened. "It isn't Kate! It's Siobhan! Get back, Sophia!"

Sophia looked down at the disc, which sat flat and unchanged, no fresh transformation wrought by Kate's touch. She stepped back, staring at her sister. At least, at the person she thought was her sister.

She was still staring when Kate hit Lucas with the kind of force that even she shouldn't have had, striking him hard enough to send him flying into the far wall.

Kate let the walls around her mind drop then, and Sophia saw that what Lucas had said was true. This wasn't Kate.

"Help!" Sophia called out. "Somebody help!"

"Shout if you want," Siobhan said, with Kate's voice. "I sent people away. I had hoped that this body's blood would be enough to fool that device, I had thought that I might be able to wait to get you alone, but it seems that my former apprentice found a way to call for help."

"Give me back my sister!" Sophia demanded.

Kate's face smiled in a way that had nothing to do with her. "She would have attacked me by now. You... the best that can be said for you is that you are a vessel for a very special child."

She raised a hand with her palm out, and Sophia didn't understand until Siobhan blew using Kate's lips, sending powder toward her in a cloud. Sophia gasped involuntarily, and felt it in her nose, her mouth, blocking the airway. She felt herself fall to her knees as weakness threatened to overwhelm her, and Kate stood there before her, looking menacing in a way that she should never have been able to manage.

"Now," Siobhan said, drawing a knife. "Hold still. We have a ritual to perform before I kill you."

CHAPTER TWENTY ONE

Cora stared out from the prow of a fast fishing boat, willing it to hurry along the fjords. She had never been beyond the Dowager's kingdom before, and if there had been more time she might have taken her time, savoring the experience. For now, though, all she wanted was for the boat to arrive in Ishjemme.

"It won't go any faster just because we want it to," Aidan said, putting a hand on her shoulder. Cora was surprised by how much that touch calmed her. There was something reassuring about having him there with her. Just not reassuring enough to completely push out the thoughts of how much danger Sophia was in.

"Sophia could be dying as we speak," Cora said. "Siobhan… you don't know how dangerous she is, Aidan."

"I've heard stories," he assured her, as Emeline came up to join them. She looked every bit as worried as Cora felt. "It's hard to guess how many of them are true."

"Probably more than we think," Emeline said. "If she's powerful enough to lock away everything Kate is like this, then she's going to be hard to deal with."

"*Can* we deal with her?" Cora asked. That worry snaked through her alongside the fear that they might be too late. What if they got there, and the thing that had imprisoned Kate was too powerful for them?

"We have to try," Emeline said. Cora would have preferred it if she'd said that yes, of course they would be able to do it. As it was, it sounded as though she was every bit as nervous as Cora felt. Cora wasn't used to Emeline being nervous about anything.

"How much further do you think it is?" Cora asked. They were sailing along fjords lined with trees, and with statues that seemed to jut out from the banks as markers. The whole place was more beautiful than she could have imagined.

"It can't be too much further," Emeline said. "I talked to the captain, and he said that on summer days, young men race up these fjords in small boats."

"Did you ask him to go as fast?" Cora asked.

Emeline smiled in reply. "Waiting is the hardest part."

For Cora, though, that wasn't quite true. Waiting wasn't the hardest part. Waiting while her friend might be dying was. If they could have sent a message ahead, she might have worried less, but like this... what if they arrived and it was already done? What if Siobhan had succeeded in killing Sophia? What if all they could do was try to save Kate from the consequences of it?

Cora knew the answer to that: they would do it. Cora might not have met Kate, but Emeline spoke about her as a friend, and that was good enough. Besides, she had to keep hope. They would go there, save Sophia, and then...

And then hope that Stonehome would allow them to return after they'd left without taking Cora's memory of it. She couldn't imagine that Asha, in particular, would be happy about that part of it.

"I think I can see the harbor," Aidan said, pointing.

Following the line of his finger, Cora could too, and it seemed busy in a way that she might not have expected. There were more ships than she expected, more men with weaponry, more boxes being loaded onto ships than taken off. It looked less like a simple city harbor and more like a place preparing for war.

"It looks like they're planning to attack somewhere," Emeline said.

Cora could think of only one place that they might attack, but it made no sense to her. Why would they attack the Dowager's kingdom? There was no obvious answer to that as their ship got closer, switching to oars to maneuver among the other vessels as it approached the shore. She looked at the town, strangely open and tree filled in comparison to the cramped confines of Ashton, trying to work out where Sophia would be. Given who she was, the castle standing above it all seemed like an obvious choice. They would be able to ask though. In all this, Cora guessed that *someone* would know where Sophia was right then.

The sailors threw down ropes, and Cora waited impatiently for them to lower a gangplank to the harbor-side. As soon as they did, Cora ran down, along with Aidan and Emeline.

"Where is Sophia?" she called out. "We have an urgent message for Sophia."

Almost instantly, it seemed, they were surrounded by soldiers with their hands on their swords. It occurred to Cora, too late, that perhaps showing up shouting in the accent of a place they might be practically at war with wasn't a good idea.

A young man stepped forward from the soldiers, and just looking at him, Cora could tell that he was someone important. He didn't look much like a soldier, but the soldiers seemed to look to him for their lead.

"I am Endi, son of Duke Lars of Ishjemme. Who are you, and what are you doing here, demanding to speak to my cousin?"

His cousin? Of course, Sophia would be his cousin if he was the son of Duke Lars. His presence was good though, because it meant that they might be able to get a warning to her in time. This might be the one way that they could speed this up, rather than having to wait.

"My name is Cora," she said. "This is Emeline, and this is Aidan. We need to warn Sophia; she's in great danger!"

"Slow down," the young man, Endi, said. "What kind of danger?"

"A witch has attacked her sister, Kate," Emeline explained, beside Cora. "She is planning to kill Sophia. Kate was able to get a warning to us, and we found a boat as fast as we could."

Cora saw Endi frown at that, obviously trying to think things through. She didn't blame him. She knew it sounded strange, but even so, they needed to hurry.

"There's no time to waste," she said. "Please, take us to Sophia. We might already be too late."

"And how do I know," Endi asked, "that you are who you say you are?"

Cora paused, frowning. She hadn't expected this, although perhaps she should have. She'd expected that people would see how important their mission was and let them through.

"Sophia can vouch for us," Emeline said. "She traveled with us."

"And conveniently, the attempt to identify you would get you close to her," Endi said. "Forgive me, perhaps you are sincere, but how are we to know that you aren't assassins, or spies sent to disrupt our preparations?"

"We're not spies!" Cora insisted, although she didn't know what good it would do. "We're trying to help!"

"Possibly that's true," Endi said, "but I think the best thing is if we take you into custody, and Sophia can decide if she wants to meet you when she has the time."

Cora could imagine what that might be like, sitting in a room somewhere, maybe for days, until someone remembered to tell Sophia what was happening. It would probably be comfortable, but it wouldn't let them deliver their message. By the point where they got to speak to their friend, it might already be too late to do anything.

"What's going on here?" a voice asked, and another young man came forward. From the first glance, it was obvious that he was Endi's brother; the similarity was too great for it to be anything else.

"Nothing for you to worry about, Jan," Endi said, in a tone that said he had everything under control.

Perhaps the other young man might have moved on at that, but Cora could see her chance. It was the only way she could avoid being a prisoner in all but name.

"Sophia is in danger," she called out. "Kate can't be allowed near her, because she isn't Kate. A witch is using her to try to kill Sophia."

It was a dangerous move. There was no reason for this young man to believe her where his brother hadn't, and shouting out like that risked annoying Endi. In fact, even as Cora said it, she could see Endi's features creasing with frustration.

"Enough," he said. "Take these three and lock them away safely. We'll deal with all this when we're not trying to put together an invasion."

"Don't be so hasty," Jan said. "If Sophia's in danger—"

"She's not, Jan," Endi said. "It's all a mistake, or a trick. Tell my brother about this warning Kate gave you."

Emeline answered. "She sent it to me, mind to mind."

The fact that Emeline was prepared to reveal that to a stranger told Cora how much she wanted to stop this from happening. She and Cora had both seen firsthand what could happen, revealing what Emeline could do.

"You have powers?" Endi said. "Maybe you're the witch trying to fool us and get to—"

Cora had put up with enough. There was no time for this. Picking a gap in the assembled soldiers, she ran into it, pulling Emeline with her. Some of them made to stop her, but Aidan was there, blocking the way.

"Go!" he yelled as men grabbed hold of him. "Warn Sophia. I'll try to hold them."

Cora felt a pang of fear for him, wondering what the soldiers there might do to Aidan, but she had to trust that he would be safe. He wasn't armed, wasn't trying to kill any of them, and once they saw that the three of them were trying to help, this would be all right.

She and Emeline raced through the streets of Ishjemme, heading upward past the houses, toward the spot where the castle stood. Behind them, soldiers ran in their wake, although Cora couldn't tell now if they were trying to chase them down, or had gotten the message that Sophia needed help.

They kept going up, and now the castle was only a short way ahead. Cora could see Emeline concentrating in the subtle way that came when she was using her powers.

"Are you trying to contact Sophia?" Cora guessed.

"I can't get through to her," Emeline said. "I hope that just means that she's distracted and not…"

She didn't have to say it. This close, if Emeline couldn't contact Sophia, it might mean something far worse. It might mean that she wasn't there to connect with anymore. At the very least, it meant that they had to hurry.

The gates to the castle lay ahead, solid looking and old-fashioned compared to the modernity of Ashton's palace. There were guards there, and Cora realized as they crossed their pikes that she hadn't thought this far ahead, didn't have a plan for getting past them. The best she could do was slam into the first of them, pushing him aside in memories of the training that she'd had with Aidan, sending him tripping to the floor. She saw Emeline doing the same with the other.

Cora slammed her fist against the wood of the door, shouting as loud as she could.

"Open up!" she yelled. "Open up! Sophia is in danger!"

From the corner of her eye, she could see the guard she'd knocked over rising, and Cora suspected that once he did, this would be over. She kept pounding on the door, and finally, almost to her shock, it opened, revealing a young woman with the same family resemblance as the two brothers back on the docks. She had a bandage on her face where she'd suffered a wound of some sort.

"What's going on?" she asked. "Why are you shouting?"

"It's Sophia," Cora said. "There's no time. If we don't get to her now, I think… I think that she's going to die!"

CHAPTER TWENTY TWO

Sophia tried to fight against the effects of the powder the witch had thrown in her face, pushing back against the urge to lie still, to sleep, to just stay there while the woman wearing Kate's body like a coat used it to murder her. No matter how much she fought, though, it wasn't enough. She couldn't move, couldn't call out for help, couldn't do anything but lie there.

"There's no point trying to fight," Siobhan said through Kate's mouth. She took out a vial of something that smelled pungent, as red as blood, so that her hands looked like a murderer's when she started to spread it on them.

She took out a knife that was inlaid with runes and knotted with sigils.

"I took this from Haxa when I killed her," Siobhan said. "The rune witch was weak and meddling, but I'm not one to turn down useful tools when they're offered. Like your sister."

She slid the knife into the fabric of Sophia's dress, and Sophia braced for the moment when it would plunge into her. Instead, Siobhan just cut it clear of the swollen skin of her belly, exposing it to the air.

Sophia tried to fight then, summoning every scrap of strength she had and trying to throw it into movement. Nothing happened.

"The powder I used will last for more than long enough for this," Siobhan said. "There's really no point in trying to do anything. You might as well lie still and let me finish this. Earn yourself a quick death."

She started to move her fingers over Sophia's belly, the red unguent on them leaving marks behind as she did it. Sophia could feel her tracing whorls and runes there, and she could feel the power that came with it.

"Wha…" Sophia managed, but it was *all* she could manage with the powder overwhelming her so completely.

"What am I doing?" Siobhan asked. "Why, I'm giving myself a new lease on life. I could stay in dear Kate's body, but I'm sure she would be executed for the murders of yourself and your brother. So it's better to kill her too, I think."

The witch paused, smearing more of the red on Sophia's stomach.

"In any case, this body is not quite designed for all that I have in mind. Why have a cast off cloak when I can tailor make one? The child you're carrying... she has *such* potential. I just need to shape her. Oh, and cut her out of you, of course."

No, Sophia wouldn't let her hurt her child. She wouldn't let this creature take her child like that. She would find a way to stop her. Except she couldn't stop her. Even as Sophia struggled to move, struggled to shout for help, Siobhan continued to draw marks on her belly.

"The runes will ease the way," Siobhan said. "So will your death. After that, I'll have a kingdom waiting for me."

"No..." Sophia managed. *Kate, fight it,* she sent, trying to get through to her sister, trying to pull her to the surface.

Siobhan laughed. "Kate is firmly imprisoned. You should blame her for this, you know. If she hadn't tried to break our pact, I wouldn't have found myself almost destroyed. I wouldn't *need* to take a body to live. I could have just kept using her to do what needed to be done, rather than all this."

If Sophia couldn't call to Kate, then there was still her brother. With an effort, she looked over to where Lucas lay, unconscious.

Wake up, she sent, *please, wake up.*

"Oh, that won't work," Siobhan said. "Given how hard I hit him, no petty human could survive. Now, shall we begin?"

She knelt by Sophia, starting to chant in words that were full of hard edges and guttural sounds. Sophia could feel the power building, could practically see it forming a web around her. That power seemed to twist and twine through her, threading into her child, despite Sophia's frantic efforts to push against it.

Siobhan lifted a knife, the blade seeming to glow with power...

...and Lucas slammed into her from the side, knocking her across the room.

"I'm not so easy to kill," he said.

Siobhan rolled to her feet. To Kate's feet. "Then I'll try harder."

She sprang at Lucas, kicking at him again. Lucas barely slipped aside in time, the blow missing him by a hair's breadth.

This time, she veered off at the last moment, heading for Sophia. She saw Lucas interpose himself, grabbing Siobhan's knife arm and wrenching the blade from it. He shoved her back, parried a kick, and took a punch on his shoulder, moving at a speed that seemed impossible.

It reminded Sophia of the fight against the Master of Crows, but this fight had none of the beauty or elegance of a sword fight. Siobhan struck out brutally with Kate's stolen flesh, lashing out with fists and feet, knees and elbows. She dove for her knife and came up with it, slashing at Lucas in a web of strikes. He parried most of them, but Sophia still gasped as she saw blood on the steel. Lucas winced and shoved Siobhan back.

He pulled out his sword, but there wasn't the shine of metal there. Instead, he kept it in its scabbard, blocking and jabbing, using it more like a club than a sword. Sophia understood the danger he faced in that moment. He was trying to fight a creature with all the speed and power that came from magic, which had no concerns about its safety, and it was inhabiting a body that Lucas couldn't risk permanently harming.

It was a task that even Lucas couldn't manage without injury. Sophia saw Siobhan lash out with the knife she held again and again, most of the blows caught by Lucas using his scabbarded sword, but some, too many, getting through. Sophia winced with every blow that landed, wishing she could do something to stop this.

She tried, throwing thought after thought at Siobhan in an effort to distract her. It felt like throwing pebbles into the ocean. Siobhan struck back, in a wave of fear and pain that had Sophia reeling. She would have screamed then if she had been able to do so. She fought through it, trying to find a way to move again, to do anything other than lie there.

Siobhan threw Lucas away from her, slamming him into the wall again, hard enough that the plaster cracked, and he brought down a tapestry as he tumbled. She lunged for Sophia, but Lucas threw the tapestry that he'd brought down like a net, catching Siobhan briefly until she cut through it with the knife she wielded. Then he was there, pulling her back even though Siobhan succeeded in cutting him as he did it.

They couldn't win like this. Siobhan only had to get to Sophia for a moment, while Lucas couldn't do anything to end the fight. Even if he did the unthinkable and thrust a sword through Kate's chest, Sophia didn't know if that would stop the creature within her. Every attempt to slow Siobhan brought some fresh blow from the witch, either drawing blood or throwing him back. Lucas had seemed unstoppable against the Master of Crows, but now Sophia couldn't see how he could win.

Siobhan threw him back again, lunging for Sophia once more. In that moment, Sophia heard the crack of the doors bursting open, and she saw the last figures she'd expected. Cora and Emeline stood there, rushing into the room together, and Cora dove at Kate's legs even as Emeline stood there, her power focusing in a way that Sophia hadn't felt before.

"You can't stop me," Siobhan said in Kate's voice, but Sophia could hear the fear and anger there.

"Grab her," Emeline yelled. "I need you to hold her!"

Guards ran in behind them, and they grabbed for Siobhan. One died as a knife found his chest, then a second found himself thrown back across the room. Lucas was there then, managing to grab Siobhan's knife arm again. A pair of guards grabbed for her other arm, and Siobhan still managed to throw one of them off.

Cora knelt by Sophia. "What has she done to you? Don't worry, I've attended to plenty of drugged noblewomen before now."

Sophia felt Emeline pushing power at Siobhan. She seemed to be lacing a net around Siobhan, locking it around the creature as it sat within Kate. Sophia could feel what her friend was trying to do, but she could also feel Siobhan pushing back, forcing Emeline's power away from her.

"Do you think this will hold me?" Siobhan demanded. She kicked out, slamming Lucas back from her. "Do you think *any* of you can hold me?"

She struck out with her knife again, and another of the guards went down, blood pouring from him. One of the men coming into the room drew a sword, and Sophia knew that if she did nothing, they would cut her sister down even as Siobhan used Kate's body to kill her.

She felt Emeline trying again, wrapping power around the immensity of Siobhan's essence. Sophia reached out, trying to help. She didn't know what Emeline was doing, couldn't do what she was doing, but she could at least try to lend her friend the power that she needed.

She felt Lucas doing the same, giving power for Emeline to direct. Sophia reached out, and in that moment she felt the kingdom around her. She felt Ishjemme, felt the land and the people, felt the power running through it. She filtered that power through herself, ignoring the sheer, uncontrollable force of it, and lending it to Emeline as best she could.

She felt Emeline shaping it, forming what had been a net into a ring of steel that tightened around Siobhan. Sophia gave her the raw materials, but Emeline forged them into something that could contain the witch's spirit. She held Siobhan there, contained within a bubble of power, even as Siobhan fought against it.

No! Siobhan screamed. *I will not be contained!*

Sophia felt Siobhan throw her power against the cage holding her. She felt the impact, but it didn't give way. She poured power into it, and it held.

Then Emeline yanked, pulling the witch from Kate's body. Sophia felt Siobhan trying to cling to her sister's body, but the cage around her gave her nothing to cling onto. Emeline pulled her clear, and for a moment, Sophia could feel the witch's spirit being held there.

For an instant, she felt a crack in that cage, and Siobhan's spirit surged forward, toward Sophia. No, not toward her. Toward her child. Instinctively, Sophia threw up defenses, throwing Siobhan back.

You can't deny me. I will not be killed!

Sophia held her ground, not letting the witch's spirit through, holding it there as Emeline wrapped it in power again. She felt the moment when Emeline took that net of power and threw it, casting what was left of Siobhan away with no home to go to. Sophia could already feel the witch's essence starting to dissolve as she tumbled away into nothingness.

Sophia opened her eyes in time to see her sister collapse, tumbling bonelessly to the ground in a tangle of limbs. Lucas was slumped, trying to stop bleeding from a dozen or more wounds. At least two guards lay dead, slaughtered in Siobhan's attack. Cora knelt over Sophia, trying to support her as whatever drug Siobhan had used worked its way through her system. All the while, Sophia stared at her sister's prone form.

They'd managed to destroy the witch, but what had it cost them?

CHAPTER TWENTY THREE

Sebastian sat in the dark, thinking of Sophia. At least, trying to think of Sophia, because she seemed like the one good thing in his life. In a place like this, clinging to thoughts of her seemed like the only way to avoid going mad. The truth, though, was that it was impossible not to think about Angelica, about Rupert, and about everything that might be happening out in the world while he was trapped beneath Rupert's townhouse.

He still couldn't believe that Angelica planned to marry his brother. It shouldn't have surprised him; he knew how ambitious Angelica was, he'd just thought... what? That she would be happy about him abandoning her? That she wouldn't seek the power that marriage to Rupert might offer? It was a foolish thought, and Sebastian pushed his attention back to Sophia. He would find a way to see her again.

He just couldn't think how he would do it.

Despair started to creep in at the edges of his mind then, pressing in the way the dark seemed to. He could endure anything so long as there was the prospect of seeing Sophia again. If there wasn't, then Sebastian wasn't sure that he could go on. The thought of never seeing his child, of never getting to tell Sophia how much he loved her... those things seemed to make his cell smaller, the world around him shrink almost to nothing. Sebastian shut his eyes in the dark and just sat there, with no way to do anything better.

In the dark, he heard the sound of the barrels by his cell being shifted back, and he opened his eyes in the expectation of whatever fresh torment Rupert or Angelica had for him. Rupert had threatened torture, while what Angelica had threatened... that might be worse in its own way. Sebastian steeled himself to fight; to at least make things difficult for them.

There was no light, though, just the click of a key turning in a lock, the person doing it obscured by the dark, making almost no noise beyond that.

"Hello?" Sebastian said. "Who's there?"

He expected Rupert to laugh then and reveal the joke, or worse, for guards to come in to grab him. Instead, the only reply was silence, and Sebastian sat there listening, hearing the pad of feet moving away from him.

"What is this?" he wondered aloud.

The obvious answer was that it was another trick, like the time they'd let him think he was escaping. Maybe they were testing if he had learned his lesson. Maybe this was a torment in itself, with the indecision that came from not knowing if there would be guards waiting just around the corner.

Maybe it would be worse than that. Maybe Rupert had found out that Angelica had visited him. Sebastian could only imagine what his brother would do then, given how quick he'd been to kill the maid who'd helped him. In spite of himself, Sebastian's fists tightened. Even though Angelica had abandoned him there, he didn't want his brother to hurt her.

"Focus," he told himself. He had to make up his mind what to do here. Should he stay still in the dark, refusing to play whatever game this was? Or would that be throwing away his one chance to get out of there?

Sebastian saw a faint flicker of light ahead now. He had to choose. He thought of Sophia, and the prospect of seeing her again. Put like that, there *was* no choice. He had to do this, even though he suspected that it wasn't real.

As quietly as he could, moving on the balls of his feet, Sebastian crept from his cell.

A candle had been set a little ways away, along with a rough-looking knife, a small pouch that clinked with coins when Sebastian lifted it, and a cloak that was rough wool, but would probably do a good job of disguising him. He took all of them, trying to work out what they meant. The knife was either a good sign or a very bad one. He didn't think Rupert would give him a weapon like that, but if he had, it meant that he was trying to play a much deadlier game than before.

Sebastian edged forward through the cellars, expecting to find guards waiting for him at any moment.

He found the first of them in the cellar, seated on a rough chair. He started at the sight of the guard, freezing in place, sure that the man must see the candlelight. When the figure didn't move, Sebastian frowned. He kept a grip on the dagger, though, every instinct telling him that this was just the precursor to some kind of attack.

It was only when he got close that he saw the man's throat had been cut.

It had been expertly done, apparently without any signs of a fight. The man didn't even have a look of surprise, as he might have if there had been even a moment to realize what was happening. It had just been one quick cut, before he could react. Sebastian looked down at the dagger in his hand, guessing now at the point of giving it to him. Any weapon was better than none, though, and it was far too late to do anything but keep going.

The next guard was at the top of the stairs leading from the cellar, just as dead as the first. His throat had been cut too, although there was something strange about the way he looked, with a purplish look to his features that suggested something more than a blade at play.

The door at the top of the stairs should have been locked, but it was just as open as the one below had been. Sebastian went out into the house. This had been the point before where guards had grabbed him, but there were none there.

He couldn't work out what game someone was playing here. It felt like a trap, yet there had been a dozen points now where someone could have sprung it if their intention had been to kill him. More to the point, why would anyone bother? If Rupert wanted him dead, he didn't need an excuse. Angelica could have sent down poisoned food. Anyone could have come with a pistol or a knife in the dark, and Sebastian couldn't have stopped them.

This was something else, but what? Who knew he was there, and what did they have to gain from letting him go like this? The fact that Angelica had found out he was there said that the secret wasn't a perfect one, and Sebastian had heard some of the people coming and going in the house. Perhaps one of them had decided to help him, or perhaps another of the servants had decided to tell someone, without risking going down to him.

Sebastian made his way through the kitchens. Those were empty. There weren't even servants to be found there, and he paused long enough to grab apples, cheese, and bread from a work surface. He felt half-starved after his ordeal in the dark.

He paused for a moment or two, trying to work out his next move. He could go through the house, looking for Rupert, or for Angelica, but what would he do then? The dagger offered one answer to that, and briefly, Sebastian held it up, considering it.

He shook his head. "I can't do it."

He couldn't go up there and confront his brother. He couldn't risk that kind of fight, and not just because Sebastian wasn't sure he would win. Even after everything Rupert had done, Sebastian couldn't imagine killing him, even in the heat of a fight. He didn't want to get out of his cell just to fight his brother. He wanted to be able to see Sophia again.

"Then I'll find a way to see her," Sebastian decided. Whatever this was, whatever reason someone had for letting him go, what he wanted from this hadn't changed. He still wanted the same thing that he'd wanted when he ran out of his wedding: he wanted Sophia.

Sebastian moved through the house, looking for a way out. Still, there were no servants, and somehow he suspected that was no accident. Either they were as dead as the guards, or someone had found a way to draw them away from the kitchens. Sebastian hoped it was the latter. He suspected that it was, because whoever had done this had left the guards where they'd killed them. Those had been a message, and perhaps the fact that they hadn't hurt the servants was a kind of message too.

He managed to find a side door. Just as with the other doors, it wasn't locked. That brought a strange feeling with it. Someone had predicted what he would do, and what path he would take. Someone had guessed his every move so far.

A part of Sebastian wanted to turn and find another exit in response to that, but there wasn't enough time. He didn't know when more guards might show up, or if whoever had set all this up might have anticipated even that move. It was better to get out of there.

Sebastian slipped out of the house, surprised to find that it was getting dark. It had been impossible to know what time it was, down in the cellar where there was no day or night. He didn't even really know how long he'd been in there.

He took a moment or two to just breathe the air of Ashton. Ordinarily, the stench of it would have been overwhelming, but after the cell, the night air felt clean and pure. Sebastian looked around, trying to get a sense of where he was.

He saw a figure in a doorway and his hand tightened on his knife, only relaxing when he saw it was just a slightly dirty-faced youth.

"You don't need to worry about me," Sebastian said. "Tell me, whereabouts in Ashton am I? Which way is it to the docks, to the palace?"

"The palace is that way," the youth said, pointing. He turned. "The docks are over there." Sebastian saw him frown. "Wait, aren't you…"

Sebastian pulled on the cloak, slipping the cowl up over his head. "I'm no one who matters," he said.

The youth shook his head. "You're Prince Sebastian."

Sebastian took a step back. "Trust me, you want to forget that I was here. There's some kind of game being played here, and you really don't want to get caught up in it."

A part of Sebastian wished that *he'd* never been caught up in it. All he'd ever wanted had been a simple life. He hadn't wanted to be caught between the pressures of what his family expected and the woman he loved. He hadn't wanted to be named his mother's heir. He certainly hadn't asked to be at the heart of the game Rupert was playing by locking him up.

Sebastian moved away down the street, coming to a spot where the road forked. The youth had been right; he could see the palace in the distance now. It would be simple to head back that way and try to tell his mother exactly what Rupert had done, and what part Angelica had played in all of it.

If he did that, though, he would be stuck there, because his mother would be careful not to let him leave again.

"I'm not going back," Sebastian said, shaking his head. He couldn't go back. He couldn't be what his mother, his family, wanted him to be. He could only try to be one thing: the kind of man who could actually be there for Sophia.

For that, he had to find a ship.

CHAPTER TWENTY FOUR

Sophia stood in the morning light, looking out over Ishjemme's harbor from a spot on top of the castle walls. The warships filled the space she could see now, ready for the invasion. Beside her, Sienne curled close, obviously unwilling to move from her side after missing the fight with Siobhan. In a way, Sophia was glad the forest cat had missed it, because she didn't want to think about what might have happened to Kate if Sienne had been there.

She turned at the sound of footsteps and saw her uncle approaching over the battlements. Lars Skyddar smiled as he approached, nodding out toward the waiting ships.

"We'll need to go down to join them soon," he said. "Unless you've changed your mind about staying behind?"

"You think that I should, don't you?" Sophia said.

"There are those who would say you had every excuse," her uncle said. "That your pregnancy will make war harder, that you've nearly been killed recently, that your sister lies unconscious, and no one could blame you for being by her side."

"But *you* don't feel that way?" Sophia asked.

Her uncle shrugged. "I can just guess how you feel in a moment like this. You feel responsible for all the men who are going to Ashton. You could no more stand back and wait for their return than I could. It's part of what makes you a good leader."

"How is Kate?" Sophia asked. "Is there any news?"

Her uncle shook his head. "She still lies asleep, but my best physikers tell me that is *all* it is. She has been through an ordeal."

"She'll be angry to miss the war," Sophia said with a smile.

Her uncle nodded at that, looking out over the city to where the boats waited. "I think we have enough people for that, though," he said. "Sophia, there's something I want to talk to you about."

That sounded serious, but then, her uncle was a serious man.

"What is it, Uncle?" she asked.

"Do you know how long we Skyddars followed your family, Sophia?" he asked. "We were dukes under them even in the days before people started to push back the magic from the lands. We used to hold our dukedom from them, renewed with each generation, even though we came to think of it as our right."

He took something out from the pocket of his greatcoat. It was a ring, set with the seal of Ishjemme. He held it out in his palm.

"I have spent the years since my wife died worrying about my children," he said. "Hans is too warlike, Endi too ready to see plots everywhere. Ulf and Freya are too wild, Oli too bookish. Jan thinks he is some hero out of legend, and Rika is too sweet to rule."

"I think my cousins are wonderful," Sophia said.

"Don't get me wrong," her uncle said, "I love my children dearly. I simply worry about what will happen when I am gone. Will they tear the family and the dukedom apart fighting over who gets what? Will one of them rule when they are not ready? You have shown that you are ready, Sophia."

"What are you saying?" Sophia asked.

"I am saying that you are like a daughter to me," Lars said. "Christina and Alfred would be proud of you if they were here. Soon, you will have a kingdom of your own, but until then, you will speak with my voice, and should anything happen to me, you will hold my seal. It will be yours to do with as you wish; to give to one of my children, or to hold, as it was in the old days."

"That's..." Sophia tried to think of the words. "It's too much. My cousins—"

"I know you won't deprive them of what is theirs," her uncle said. "You'll do better. You'll give them a whole country in which they can seek new fortunes. And, if one of them should become the right person to be duke or duchess here, that will be your choice."

"You're hoping that I'll decide for you," Sophia guessed.

Her uncle nodded. "Forgive a father for not wanting to choose between his children. And, in the meantime, it means that my dukedom will be in safe hands. Will you do it? We have already accepted you as our queen, but will you be my heir as well?"

Sophia could see how much it meant to him. It meant safety and certainty for Ishjemme. It gave her the same, because for all that they'd acknowledged her queen of the Dowager's kingdom, there wouldn't be any power with that until they succeeded in conquering it.

Sophia reached out and, very carefully, picked up the seal.

"I'll try to be worthy of it," she said.

Her uncle nodded. "I have no doubt that you will be. Now, I'm going to go down to join the ships. Don't be long. You have a kingdom to retake."

***

Sophia felt her brother's arrival before she saw him coming up onto the battlements. To her surprise, Sienne ran to Lucas, then hurried back, wrapping around her legs again.

We'll need to go soon, he sent across to her.

Soon, Sophia agreed, then switched to speaking aloud. "How are your wounds?"

"They'll heal," Lucas assured her. "Nothing seems to be slowing me down. What about you? Any aftereffects from the poison?"

Sophia shook her head. "My main worry is what all this might have done to my daughter."

"She'll be fine and strong, like her mother," Lucas said.

"Like her aunt, maybe," Sophia said.

Lucas stood in silence for a moment or two. "Is that why you're delaying before going? Are you hoping that Kate is going to wake up and join us?"

It was perceptive, although Sophia suspected that their connection probably helped with that part of things. She leaned on the parapets.

"Yes," she said. "I think I am. I know it's stupid. I shouldn't be wishing that my sister would wake up so that I can drag her off to war. It's just… we've spent enough time apart. I want her there."

"I can understand that," Lucas said. "From the moment I learned of you and Kate, it was like there was a hole in me that I hadn't known existed. I had to find you."

"And you did," Sophia said. "I just wish we'd been able to make that device of yours work. It's another thing we'll need Kate for."

Assuming that she ever woke up. In spite of what her uncle's physikers might say, Sophia was sure that no one should sleep like this. What if there was some damage in the wake of the battle with Siobhan? What if her sister was whole in body, but not in mind? What if—

"I believe that Kate is all right," Lucas said. "When she gave me her warning, I felt the strength of her essence. She will be awake soon enough."

"And probably getting into the kind of fights that make me wish she were safely asleep," Sophia said.

"Probably," Lucas agreed. He reached out to put a hand on Sophia's shoulder. "You know that we can't wait any longer. You want to go and rescue this prince of yours? Well, we should do that before anything can happen to him."

Sophia knew that everything her brother was saying made sense. If Sebastian was in danger, then it made no sense to delay even a moment longer than necessary. Even so, she couldn't shake the hope that Kate would walk onto the rooftop at any moment to join them.

"We'll do this," Lucas said, "come back, and she'll be waiting for us safely."

Sophia liked the sound of that. Maybe this was the way of doing this where Kate stayed the safest. Maybe she would wake to a world where the Dowager had already been overthrown, Sebastian was free, and all that was left to do was find their parents. Maybe Kate wouldn't have to risk her life the way she had so many times. That was a good thought.

"Come on," Sophia said, "let's go."

She made her way with Lucas down through the castle. The chaos of the last little while had slowed, so that it might have seemed peaceful if Sophia didn't know it was because everyone was waiting with the ships, ready to go to war. Only a few were being left behind: Sophia saw Rika waving to her and waved back, while Oli seemed to be coordinating a dozen things at once, trying to keep things together with his books and his papers.

I'm doing the right thing, aren't I? Sophia asked her brother, not daring to say it aloud.

You're acting out of love, Lucas said. *That's a better reason than birthright, or honor, or the desire for power. If you won't change the world for someone you love, what will you do it for?*

Sophia nodded, determined now. She and Lucas made their way down through Ishjemme, and in spite of the fact that she had only been there a short while, it already felt like home. She would miss it while she was gone.

By the time they reached the docks, the last of the ships was loaded. They flew their flags, pennants fluttering in messages to one another. Sophia went to her uncle's flagship, a long, slender vessel named the *Briar* with cannon running along the sides. She made her way up the gangplank and found the sailors there waiting for her, standing straight.

They're waiting for you to speak, Lucas said.

Sophia nodded, looking around at the men.

"This was something I hadn't wanted to do," she said. "I thought that it was stupid, going to fight just so that I could sit on a throne rather than the Dowager. This is about more than that, though. It is about safety for all of us, when an enemy sits across the water who would kill us given any opportunity. It is about justice for those they have already killed, on the night when they slaughtered so many people."

She paused, thinking for a moment about the way Lucas had put it.

"It's about love," Sophia said. She pointed. "The man I love sits across the water, languishing in a cell. His mother is a ruthless tyrant, his brother is worse. It is a land where those like me are hunted and killed, where people are sold like chattel and killed in the wars of the nobles. It's a place where people who argue are killed or driven out onto the fringes, into the hills and the mountains, the moors and the forests."

She shook her head.

"It's time for that to change," she said. "We'll change it. We're going to take the kingdom back, and we're going to do it for everyone. We're going to do it because if we stand by any longer, we're condemning innocent people, not just Sebastian, but everyone oppressed there. We're going to do it because it's the right thing to do."

Around her, the men cheered and thumped their fists on the ship's woodwork. Sophia moved to the prow of the ship while they started to set the *Briar* into motion. It started to slide through the water, and behind Sophia, the whole fleet followed.

"Hold on, Sebastian," she whispered. "We're coming."

CHAPTER TWENTY FIVE

Kate felt herself coming back to wakefulness like a swimmer rising from deep water, floating up one phase at a time, through blackness into grays and then into the light. It seemed to take forever before her eyes flickered open, and when they did, she gasped with the effort of it.

"Easy, Kate. You've been through a lot." A woman leaned over her, holding a cup of water to her lips.

"Careful, Cora," a young man said from the other side of the room. "You don't know for sure that it's her."

Emeline was there with him, playing a game involving bone dice. "It's her, Aidan. The witch is gone."

Gone. Kate paused at that thought, looking down deep inside of herself, trying to find any trace of Siobhan left inside her. There was nothing, not just of Siobhan, but nothing. Kate felt scoured clean; empty. She wasn't sure what it all meant.

She did know one thing. She was free, in a way she hadn't truly been before. She'd been an orphan first, and then Siobhan's apprentice. There had always been someone with some kind of claim on her. Now, for the first time, there wasn't.

Kate could feel tears of happiness building in her eyes at that thought.

"I… you saved me," Kate managed. Memories of the place she'd been trapped flared up in her mind, and she winced at them. She told herself that she was free of it, that it was gone, but even so, she guessed that those memories would be with her for a long time to come.

"We wouldn't have been able to if you hadn't called to us," Emeline said. "I heard you shouting from across the distance of the sea."

"And you came," Kate said, sitting up. "Came to help me."

"Well, you and Sophia," Emeline said. She gestured to the other young woman there. "This is Cora. She and I traveled with Sophia across most of the kingdom. And that's Aidan, from Stonehome."

"You *found* Stonehome?" Kate said. When they'd been on the barge together, Emeline had mentioned her dream of finding somewhere safe, but Kate hadn't been sure if it even existed. That they'd found it seemed incredible.

"We did," Cora said. She frowned for a moment. "I hope we'll still be able to go back when this is done."

"Why wouldn't you?" Kate asked.

Emeline answered that. "We left in kind of a hurry to help you. Without asking permission."

Kate stared at them. If that was true, then the three of them had potentially given up an incredible amount in order to help her. Kate could barely believe that someone would cross the sea to try to save her and Sophia, but to do it knowing that they might not be able to go back?

"There will be a home for you in Ishjemme," she promised. "If you can't go back to Stonehome, I'll make sure of it."

She would do it even if she had to build them one herself, although Kate doubted it would come to that. Sophia had every reason to be grateful toward them as well.

"If Aidan here is from Stonehome," she said, "does that mean that he has the same gifts as us?"

She tried sending a message over in Aidan's direction, and was surprised when nothing happened. It wasn't just that she didn't get a response; Kate knew what that felt like, and this was more than that. She felt blank inside, empty.

Tentatively, she stood up, ignoring Cora's attempts to push her back down. Even that was harder than it should have been. She didn't have the strength or the speed that she should have possessed, didn't have the power of the magic flowing through her muscles. Experimentally, Kate took her sword from where it lay on a dresser close to the bed and tried a few lunges with it. The results were disappointing. She still knew how to do it, still had every subtlety of swordplay locked inside her mind, but there was no extra force there, no special speed. She tried reaching out for Cora's mind, and there was nothing for her to reach with.

Her powers were gone.

Kate stood there, very still, trying to make sense of it. The idea that the powers she'd lived with her whole life might be gone was… well, it was shocking.

"Are you all right, Kate?" Cora asked.

To her own surprise, Kate nodded.

"I'm fine," she said.

It was even true. What did it matter if she'd lost her powers, if that was what it cost for her to finally be free? What had they ever allowed her to do, except kill people? If she hadn't gone looking for the ability to fight better than anyone else, she would never have met Siobhan, and she might still have been back at Thomas's forge with Will.

She'd only ever wanted to be free. The skills to fight, the use of her powers... all of that had been to stop anyone else from being able to control her, yet all that she owed Siobhan for those powers had *been* what had controlled her, in the end. Now, she was free of it. She was better off.

"Are you *sure* you're OK?" Emeline said. *You seem a little strange.*

Kate heard the words at least, but she knew she wouldn't be able to send anything back.

"I'm fine," she repeated. "I'm not still possessed by a witch, if that's what you're worrying about. I'm just getting used to being back in my own body."

She stretched her arms out, feeling the push of them through the air. The place that Siobhan had kept her felt real enough, but there was still a difference between that and the subtle drift of breeze across her skin where the shutters were open.

"I think I want to take a walk," she declared, more on a whim than anything.

Cora put a hand on her shoulder. "You should lie back down. You're still recovering."

"How long was I asleep?" Kate asked.

Emeline answered. "Most of a day."

"Then I think I've been lying down enough, don't you?" she countered. She smiled at their disapproving looks. "I'm grateful for all you've done," she said. "I am, but I'm free for just about the first time in my life, and I don't want to waste that time confined to my bed. Come with me if you want to make sure that nothing will happen, but I'm taking a walk. I'm going to find my sister."

"Kate..." Emeline began, but Kate had already set off, making her way out from her rooms and down into the castle. She wanted to find Sophia. More than that, she wanted to find the brother whose mind she had touched, but whom she had never met in the flesh. She wanted to find Lucas and thank him for saving Sophia.

She headed through the castle with the others hurrying along somewhere behind her, trying to keep up. In spite of everything that had happened to her, Kate felt as though she could happily run through the halls without effort, so she did. There didn't seem to be as many people around as usual, so there was almost no one to crash into on her way down toward the great hall.

Kate ran in there and the few guardsmen who were there reached for their weapons on reflex, obviously still remembering who she'd been. Kate raised her hands.

"I'm me again, I promise," she said. "Where's Sophia?"

"Kate?"

Kate looked round and found her cousin Rika approaching. Rika hugged her, and that seemed to put even the guards at ease.

"I'm so glad you're all right," Rika said.

Kate smiled at that. "I'm more than all right. "Where is Sophia?" she asked, looking around. "Where's my brother? I want to meet him."

Rika stepped back, shaking her head. "They aren't here, Kate."

Kate frowned at that. "What do you mean, they aren't here? Did something happen to them? Did I… did I hurt them?"

"No," Rika said quickly, reaching out to take her hand. "Nothing like that. Sophia has gone to see to the preparations for the invasion, Kate. Lucas has gone with her. You were asleep so long that they didn't think you'd be awake for it."

Kate frowned. "What invasion? What is Sophia doing?"

"She's planning to invade the Dowager's kingdom," Rika said.

"To string the old hag up by her throat for all she's done to us?" Kate asked.

Her cousin shook her head. "To save Sebastian. The Master of Crows told her that Sebastian was imprisoned in Ashton. It's very romantic, when you think about it."

Rika was probably the only one of the cousins who would think about it that way. Kate certainly didn't.

"She's going all that way, taking all those risks, for *Sebastian*?"

"Well," Rika said, "she said it was better to have an invasion that was about love than one for some other reason."

"But that's stupid!" Kate said. "She doesn't think straight when it's about him, and he's done nothing but hurt her. And going off somewhere because the Master of Crows says something is crazy! I've fought him. He wouldn't do anything without his own reasons."

Kate could guess what some of those reasons might be too. The man, the *thing*, she'd fought on the continent's beaches lived for carnage. An invasion now would give him more of that while leaving Ishjemme weakened.

Rika shrugged. "Probably, but the invasion is still set now. Almost everyone is going. Oli and I are the only ones of my family who aren't joining it, and that's just because Father says we have to stay here to look after Ishjemme. Even Endi has gone, and I'd have thought he could have done half the things he does from here, sending messages."

Kate tried to think it through, but what was there to think about? If Sophia was about to go running off back to Ashton, then Kate knew where she needed to be, and it was right by her sister's side. She turned, finding Cora, Emeline, and Aidan waiting at the entrance to the great hall.

"Kate," Emeline said. "Sophia wanted you to rest. She wanted you to be safe."

Kate shrugged. "My sister knows me better than that, Emeline. You should too."

"I do," Emeline said, "but how do you even expect to catch up to her? She left for the docks an hour ago."

"Ships take time to sail," Kate said, with the certainty of someone who had traveled to war with Lord Cranston's company. "Warships more than most. The ships won't depart until every last provision is lashed down, every last soldier checked."

She had to convince herself of that. It was the only option that gave her enough time to find her sister and her brother, to unite with them for all of this. Maybe she could even get there in time to talk Sophia out of leaving Ishjemme defenseless just so that she could run around after Sebastian, or at least convince her that killing the Dowager was their real priority.

Taking a breath, Kate ran from the hall. She didn't have the inhuman speed that Siobhan's fountain had lent her, but she could still run, could still sprint her way to the docks and make certain that she didn't miss the battle.

CHAPTER TWENTY SIX

Endi stood aboard one of the warships toward the side of the line, watching the progress of the fleet toward Ashton. Even he had to admit that it was impressive. Somehow, Sophia had managed to bring together clans from Ishjemme and beyond for her war, in a collection that looked as though it could sweep through almost any foe.

Endi knew as well as anyone that appearances could be deceptive, though.

"This is madness," he whispered, but he *kept* it to a whisper. It was the kind of thing that could mean trouble for him. He couldn't let people see his dissatisfaction; not if he was going to do anything about it.

The size of the fleet was impressive, but Endi knew the kind of forces that the Dowager had been able to bring to bear in the past. He'd seen the ships that the Master of Crows had brought, too. Compared to that, was it really so impressive?

Even if they won, even if somehow they pushed past Ashton's defenses, too many of Ishjemme's people would die doing it. Couldn't they see that? Apparently not. Endi had heard the way they'd all cheered for Sophia's scheme. He'd cheered with them. He knew better than to be the one person not shouting approval around a would-be ruler.

A deeper anger burned in him too. He'd seen a flash of his father's signet ring on Sophia's finger. That ring should have been his. He was the son who actually arranged things and made them happen. He wasn't silly, like Rika, or warlike, like Hans. He wasn't too bookish or too obsessed with hunting, didn't spend all his time trying to be a hero, either. It seemed obvious to him that he should have been the one speaking with his father's voice.

"This isn't about me," Endi said to himself. "This is about Ishjemme."

There was no doubt in his mind that this invasion would hurt his homeland and its people. There was the obvious point that many of them would die in the violence that was to follow. Then there was the likelihood that the Dowager would counterattack in the wake of the invasion's failure, ceasing to ignore the dukedom the way she had through the rest of her reign. Added to that, there was the more serious threat posed by the Master of Crows, who was presumably just waiting for Ishjemme to weaken both itself and its foe before resuming his campaign of conquest.

Put like that, this was more than madness. It was a form of treason against Ishjemme. And for what? So that Sophia could go to rescue her lover? So that she could rescue the Dowager's *son*? Given all the cruelties their family had inflicted, wouldn't they be better off leaving him to die, and then using it as just more proof of the Dowager's tyranny?

To him, all of this was proof of one thing: Sophia wasn't fit to lead Ishjemme.

Endi started to move across the ship, writing a note to send with a bird. They only had doves for this journey, fearful that any raven or crow might be controlled. He set it carefully on the bird's leg, then set it winging away, traveling back in the direction of Ishjemme.

"Sending messages back to Rika, brother?" Jan said, coming up to join him. "Trying to make sure she does everything just the way you would want?"

"Something like that," Endi said with an easy smile that matched Jan's. The difference was that, as far as Endi could see, his brother didn't have to work at it. It just came naturally.

"You could have stayed home," Jan said. "You could have sent your birds from Ishjemme."

"And miss out on the glory?" Endi countered, ignoring the part where his brother didn't really have a clue what it was that he did. A war could be won or lost by intelligence, and Jan thought he could help with it from across the sea? "I'll leave it to Rika and Oli, I think."

Let them stay behind where they couldn't influence anything. It wasn't as though they were siblings who had a chance to make a name for themselves as Duke. Now, if *Jan* had stayed behind, Endi might have been worried, but his brother wasn't going to stray as far from Sophia as that.

"Rika is stronger than she looks," Jan said. "But you know that, you saw her part in saving Sophia from that guardsman."

Endi nodded, trying to hide his annoyance. If his sister hadn't been there, Bjornen might have finished the job, and none of this would have come to pass. Endi simply hadn't been able to stand by and let the assassin murder his sister along with Sophia. This was about *saving* his family, not killing them.

"She is," he agreed. "Although I don't know if the guardsman was as dangerous as that thing controlling Kate. Do you think we've just left Rika there with it without knowing?"

If he could give his brother a reason to go home, then all the better. Although thoughts of it still brought a hint of annoyance to Endi. He'd tried to delay Sophia's would-be rescuers, and they'd still gotten there in time. It would all have been simpler if she'd died. She would have been gone, the invasion would have been prevented, and her sister would have been locked away where she couldn't do any harm.

"Think what it will be like," Jan said. "We will have our family's lands back across the water when this is done."

"Oh, I'm thinking about it," Endi assured him.

Mostly, he was thinking about what it would take to stop it all. They were lands that they hadn't seen in their lives, and that would probably mean fresh fights against whoever currently occupied them. Endi wondered sometimes if his brother could really see the world so simply, without any of the consequences that dogged his every thought.

"You worry too much about things, Endi," Jan said, clapping him on the shoulder.

Endi smiled at that. His brother truly meant it, he knew. "And you don't worry enough, Jan. Still, don't worry, I'll be there to cover your back when you charge in without thinking to impress Sophia."

"I'm not trying to impress Sophia," Jan said, a little too hotly.

"Of course you aren't," Endi said. "Now, I'd best go. I've more messages to write if all this is going to go smoothly."

His brother could have asked what messages. Endi would have, but Jan wasn't him. He trusted too much. He wasn't even watching Endi as Endi made his way across the deck, in the direction of one of the clan leaders. Endi knew that because he *was* watching, making sure that his brother didn't see anything he shouldn't.

"My lord Skyddar," the man said, with a nod of respect.

"Torst," Endi said, with a nod that matched it. He clasped the man's hand the way a brother might. "You're coming a long way across the sea with us for this."

"Aye, it is a journey," the other man agreed.

They sat there for a while, staring out at the sea. Endi was good at talking, but he knew when not to talk, too. A man like this wouldn't respect someone who said too much at a time.

"It will be a long journey back, too," Endi said, "if the Master of Crows attacks."

The other man frowned for a moment or two, then nodded. "Aye, it could be."

"And all your men are here, a part of this," Endi said. "Who's tending the home fires now, Torst?"

"My wife is there, and my youngest boy," the clan leader said.

"Doesn't seem like enough somehow, if men come while we're gone."

Endi paused again, letting the other man think about that for a while.

"Aye," Torst admitted, "it's a thought."

Endi sighed. "Why are you a part of this, Torst?"

The other man shrugged. "Why wouldn't I be?"

"You just told me that," Endi said. "You've a wife at home and a son. You must have something special ahead of you to send you racing into battle like a man half your age."

"I'd have thought you'd be happy of it," the other man said, spitting out over the side of the boat. "It's your family taking us there for this."

"My *cousin*," Endi said, stressing the word. "And I fear the harshness of her life has given her some strange ideas about how the world works. She thinks that if we all charge over to Ashton, they'll lay down their arms and we'll roll over them."

"Whereas you don't think it will be so easy?" Torst asked.

Endi looked at him for long seconds. He took out a flask of wine, handing it to the other man. "Did you ever hear of a war that worked like that? I haven't."

"No," Torst said. He took a sip of the wine. "Wars are a bloody business. Nothing neat or easy about them."

"And even if you win, you're likely to spark another, half the time," Endi said. "I've read about the civil wars. I've no wish to be part of another set of them. It might be better to avoid it completely."

The look Torst gave him was a hard one, but Endi had been expecting a look like that at some point. The other man was a clan leader, after all, and you didn't get to be *that* without some pride.

"I'm no coward," Torst said.

"Do you think I am?" Endi countered, his hand straying to the hilt of his sword. "A man should have the strength to fight for his home, his family. And here we are, sailing further from both. For what? Some fool's errand to save a man whose family has stood as enemies to ours for generations?"

He let those words sink in; could practically see Torst thinking.

"You've a point, but what you're hinting at… men could call it treason too."

Endi shook his head. "Treason is betraying your home, your kingdom. This is being ready to save it. I'm not asking you to run away for no reason. I'm just asking you to pull back if it looks as though we're going to be left with no one to defend Ishjemme, no one to keep our people safe."

With another man, he might have offered money. With other men, he *had* offered money. For Torst, though, that wasn't the way. A man like him would be insulted by it.

"You're saying that it might not even come to it?" Torst said.

Endi shrugged. "I'm not such a fool as to throw away a safe victory," he said. "But if I hear reports of danger, we must be ready to hurry home to meet it. Will you be ready to move if I send the message?"

He didn't call it an order. A man like this would heed a warning where he wouldn't follow a command.

"Aye," Torst said. "I'll be ready."

Endi clasped the man's hand again, thinking of all the other hands he had clasped in the last few days. Sometimes gold had changed hands, sometimes promises of power. Sometimes he had spoken about honor, or protecting their families. Endi said whatever he needed to say to ensure that they would act when the time came.

Ishjemme was in peril, even if he was the only one who could see it. He couldn't charge in to save it with a sword, but he could protect it, from anything, and *anyone,* who threatened it.

CHAPTER TWENTY SEVEN

Lord Cranston and his men sailed for Ishjemme with all the speed that their borrowed boats would allow. He wished that speed were greater, but it turned out that a man betraying his queen's commands couldn't afford to be picky, and there were only so many vessels that would take them where they wanted to go.

He gripped the side rail tight as they approached the fjords, thinking of how this would look to anyone there on the shore. He wasn't surprised to find fires springing up on the shore, warning signals telling the city beyond that they were coming.

"They think that we're enemies, my lord," Will said, moving to Lord Cranston's side. Lord Cranston didn't mind the familiarity of it. Will was probably the only person in their company who missed Kate more than him, and he was a capable lad, useful to have around.

"Wouldn't you?" Lord Cranston replied. "When a free company comes calling uninvited, it typically means blood."

Eventually, this visit would probably mean blood too, but for the Dowager, not for Kate or her people. Lord Cranston was no less determined now than he had been at the start of this voyage: he would serve Kate in whatever conflict was coming. It was the first time that Lord Cranston had felt this right about a job, even if there was no commission, no certainty of payment, perhaps even no real hope of winning.

He drummed his fingers on the rail of the ship, both impatient to get to Ishjemme and thinking about the potential consequences of those fires.

"Tell the men that I don't want any signs of weapons on deck," he said. "Get the captain to fly a flag of parley, and signal all but the lead ship to hang back."

"Yes sir," Will said, hurrying off to do it. Not quite with the speed that Kate had once done it, but still good enough. Pennants flew up the lines of their ship, giving orders. Their ship moved on ahead of the others with them, and when small boats came out to guide them through the shallows, Lord Cranston waved to them.

"Ahoy there! I am Lord Peter Cranston. We have come to join the Danse sisters' forces."

"We've no need of mercenaries," a man shouted up from one of the boats.

Lord Cranston looked him up and down. "I didn't know sailors made those decisions. I'm here to speak to the sisters."

"You'll have enough trouble with that," the man said, but even so, his small boat started to guide them in toward the shore. Lord Cranston just hoped that he would do it honestly, because some of the rocks there looked as though they could tear a ship to shreds with ease.

They went forward, and the moment Lord Cranston saw the city of Ishjemme, his heart fell. He'd been expecting a wall of warships getting ready to fight, a city with soldiers everywhere he looked and cannon bristling. Now though, even with the warning fires burning, only a small contingent of soldiers stood ready to meet them on the docks. The water in front of them was almost empty, any ships that had been there long gone.

"We're too late," Lord Cranston said.

They'd missed it. They'd missed the invasion.

***

Will stared at Ishjemme as their ship creaked its way to its docks, feeling somehow empty as they got close to it. He'd been expecting… well, he'd been expecting *more*, he guessed. He'd been expecting there to be a fleet there, for there to be soldiers…

For Kate to be there.

Lord Cranston gestured to him as they bumped against the docks, and Will went over to them with him, hopping to them and feeling the unsteadiness after his legs had only just gotten used to the rolling of the sea.

There were soldiers there waiting, headed by a young man who looked as though he would rather have been reading in a library somewhere. He didn't even wear a sword, yet the men there were looking to him, waiting for him to say something.

"I should warn you," he said, "that Ishjemme's port regulations are quite strict on the subject of pirates, bandits, and raiders."

He said it so blandly that Will almost missed the threat in it.

"Then it is a good thing that we are none of those things," Lord Cranston said. "I am Lord Peter Cranston, and you, I believe, are Oli Skyddar."

Will was impressed by that, even though he should have guessed that Lord Cranston would have made preparations for anything he might encounter in Ishjemme. Of course he would have learned what he could about Duke Lars's family.

"Lord Cranston?" Oli said. "You were the one whose company Kate fought in."

"I was," Lord Cranston said, and Will felt some of the tension leaving the situation. "She was like a daughter to me, and I came here to join her, to fight alongside her. I see I am too late."

Too late. The words still hurt Will. He'd hoped that he would see Kate again. He'd hoped… he'd hoped all kinds of things. When she'd left, he'd felt so empty, and then when Lord Cranston had announced that they were going to serve her sister, he'd dared to hope again. The thought that they'd missed her felt like a blade thrust into his heart.

"I'm sorry," Oli said. "The fleet has already sailed for Ashton, with most of my family, and Sophia, aboard."

"Sophia?" Will said. "Not Kate?"

He blurted it out before he could think to do otherwise. Both Lord Cranston and the bookish-looking young man turned to him and Will winced at the sudden attention.

"Sorry," he said. "It's just that… I was hoping to see her."

"We all were, Will," Lord Cranston said.

"That might still be possible," Oli said, and just those words were enough to send fresh hope burning through Will's heart. "Once she recovers."

"Recovers?" Will blurted. Even after the last outburst, he couldn't help it. "Kate's hurt?"

From the worried look that crossed Lord Cranston's face, he wanted to blurt out the same thing, although he managed to control himself.

"There was an attack," Oli began. "Kate was—"

Will wasn't paying attention at that point, because he was too busy watching the quartet of figures running down through the city. Three of them, two young women and a man, ran along together, while at the head of them…

"Kate!" Will shouted as she got closer. He ran to meet her, and damn the discipline of a military company. She stopped as he ran to her, and Will drew her into his arms without even thinking about it. It was so natural to kiss her then, so obvious, and he did it, clinging to her, not wanting to let her go because he suspected that the moment he did it, whatever dream this was would disappear.

Lord Cranston's cough reminded him that they were a long way from alone. Will pulled back, staring at Kate, trying to drink in every hint of difference, every change in her.

140

"Kate, are you all right? They said you were recovering from something. Did something hurt you?"

Whatever it was, he swore in that moment that he would destroy it. Then he laughed to himself. Kate didn't need his help in fighting *anything.*

Kate shook her head. "That's all done with, Will. I'm so glad to see you again." She seemed to remember the presence of the others there, pulling back. "There's so much I need to say to you, but later, all right?"

"Later," Will agreed. Somehow, it always seemed to be later, but if that kiss was anything to go by, he couldn't object to the promise of it.

"Oli," she said. "Am I too late? Are they all gone?"

The young man at the head of the soldiers nodded. "I was just telling Lord Cranston here that. They left for Ashton an hour before we sighted Lord Cranston's ships, at least."

Will saw Kate turn to Lord Cranston then, and for a moment he thought that perhaps she might hug him. Instead, she saluted.

"Generally," Lord Cranston said, in a serious tone, "the penalty for desertion is execution."

Will froze at that, fear building inside of him. Surely Lord Cranston couldn't mean that? The man was mercurial, occasionally severe, always prickly, but something like that would be… insane.

"In this case, though," Lord Cranston said, "I'll settle for you accepting my company as yours, Kate."

He dropped to one knee, holding up his sheathed sword for her to take. Will copied the movement, and around him, he saw the rest of Lord Cranston's company doing the same. From what he understood, they'd come there with the intention of serving Sophia, but she wasn't here, and Kate was. More than that, Kate was the one who had served with them, fought with them, saved them.

Kate was the one he loved, even as he felt all kinds of other things about her running away so suddenly.

Will saw Kate move to Lord Cranston, taking his sword and then handing it back to him.

"I'm not a queen," Kate said, "and you taught me to always ask when you were being paid for fighting. I'm not sure we have much to offer."

"You have more than enough," Lord Cranston assured her. Will could only agree with it.

Kate nodded. "I'll accept your help on Sophia's behalf. There's one condition though."

"What condition?" Lord Cranston asked.

"I'm told that there's a war on," Kate said. She nodded to the ship that sat there. "I don't know about you, but I'd like to join it."

CHAPTER TWENTY EIGHT

The Master of Crows let his attention wander, splitting it through bird after bird as he watched the events unfolding below. He let his borrowed eyes take in an execution in Heimdorf, a meeting along a riverbank. He collected pieces to fit together like a master craftsman inlaying a table, the pattern of it already forming in his head.

All of that was a distraction, though, a way of ensuring that nothing unexpected happened. The part that mattered, he watched with corvid after corvid, raven and crow, rook and magpie, all watching fragments of the whole.

He brought his attention back, briefly, to the grand house in Carrick where he sat in the drawing room, maps spread out on a table. Wooden pieces sat there, moved by junior officers according to the latest reports. The Master of Crows looked through the eyes of one of his creatures, reached out, and corrected the position of one of them by the width of a finger.

"The report is old," he said, "and they were deceived. Tell the scout to take more care next time."

"Yes, my lord," a junior officer said.

Only then did the Master of Crows turn his attention to the more senior officers standing waiting near the door. He watched them talking among themselves for a moment or two, seeing the latest rounds of friendships and petty rivalries. When he gave them his full attention, they fell as silent as penitents in one of the Masked Goddess's temples.

"How is the recovery from our invasion of the Dowager's lands going?" he asked.

"Well, my lord," one of the captains said, "we have sent out recruiting parties for more men."

"The foundries work day and night to produce cannon," another said, as if trying to outdo the first of them.

"Our shipmasters have commandeered vessels to replace those lost."

They sounded as though they were trying to outdo one another in begging for his favor. Idly, the Master of Crows wondered if he should show some arbitrary sign of it to one of them, to stoke whatever jealousy lay between them. His crows told him which had cheated the others at cards, which was sleeping with another man's wife. It would be an easy thing to stoke those resentments into anger. Perhaps a duel would result, and his crows would feast.

No, that would be a petty meal, and would cause too much disruption in his armies at a point where a far greater one was in the offing.

"You have done well then," he said instead, the praise spread evenly for once. "I want our men ready to move at my command."

"Yes, my lord," they chorused.

Another man might have felt some pride at the feat of bringing men from so many different lands and factions together. His New Army had quashed the rivalries of the past, and could have paved the way for a brighter future for the world, if the Master of Crows had any interest in such things. He'd taken them and honed them into a single blade of many interlinked leaves; something that could be wielded with precision, rather than some clumsy collection of butcher's knives.

"See that you are," he warned them. "I will not miss the moment to act because you are too slow."

That was the risk with any force this size. His birds could show him anything he chose to look at, but how quickly could men respond when he required it? The speed with which he could see events or have mynah birds caw commands was sometimes nothing more than a reminder of how slow things were.

He watched the men leave, hurrying back to their posts with a renewed sense of purpose. For his part, the Master of Crows seated himself in a high-backed chair, getting ready to renew his watch over events.

To his surprise, one of the junior officers chose that moment to speak up.

"My lord," he asked, "do you think that we will ever be done with war? Do you think that we will ever finally win and go home?"

The others there shrank back from him, as if expecting their commander to jump up and kill the young man at any moment. Perhaps there were days when the Master of Crows might have, but today was not one of them.

"No, Clancel, I do not."

Perhaps the young officer started at the use of his name, although it was no great feat to remember who his subordinates were. Perhaps he started at the fact that he was getting an answer at all. Either way, the shock seemed to embolden him.

"But, my lord, why not? Surely there must come a point where we have defeated all our enemies?"

The Master of Crows shook his head. "There will always be fresh enemies, fresh threats to our way of life. We must be vigilant against them. Indeed, peace would be bad for us. Peace breeds complacency and weakness. It is the phase where a nation grows no stronger, and prepares to slide into its dotage."

They were well-rehearsed arguments, convincing to young men, spouted by the old as justifications for the battles of their youth. A whim struck the Master of Crows. Ordinarily, he did not act on whims, but in this quiet moment, he could see no harm in it.

"Clancel, what would you do if I told you that everything I have just said was an utter lie?" he demanded.

"My lord?" the young officer asked, in that tone men had when they didn't want to answer.

"You heard what I said," the Master of Crows replied. "Everything I have just told you is a lie. It is a move in a game, designed to motivate you to renewed efforts."

To his credit, Clancel did his best. "Then I would have to ask what this game is, my lord, and what its purpose can be if it is not victory."

The Master of Crows considered it for a moment, and then nodded. "The game is one that a man like you could never understand. That is not an insult, I do not pick stupid men for my officers, but this is too far from any normal man's experience. People talk of chess, but what are three dozen pieces compared to those a real commander juggles?"

"The game is war?" Clancel asked, but then shook his head. "No, my lord, I could understand war. If you are talking of something more…"

He almost seemed to grasp it. As the Master of Crows had said, he did not make stupid men officers. The truth was that understanding the full scope of this game required more than intelligence. It required the skill to see the possibilities in small actions, the understanding of the way the world could turn and be turned. In a way, the destruction of the woman of the fountain made the world a poorer place for that. She had been one person who could truly appreciate the game's scope.

Still, the Master of Crows decided to try. "The game is not war, not even power, but life and its control. All of it. Every moment is a struggle. There is pain and death throughout this world, and the only strength that matters is that needed to go on. The wars will not end, because they feed my crows and make me stronger. You will die, Clancel, eventually. All of you here in this room will, and I will not. And that is the whole of it."

The men there stared at him as if he were mad, so he laughed then, making the whole thing into some grand joke. He laughed, and the men there laughed with him, because they did not wish to believe it, because the truth could no more be stared at than the sun.

"Forgive me, Clancel," he said, "I am in a mood to jest with you today. The wars are harsh, but they are necessary, and sometimes men must remember to laugh, or they will go mad with it."

For a moment, the junior officer stared at him with a thoughtful look. For the briefest moment, the Master of Crows thought that he would have the strength of will to see through it, to hold to the burning flame of it all, but no, he nodded.

"Thank you, my lord."

The Master of Crows nodded to the table. "You should shift that piece the width of a nail to the north. The troops there have moved."

He left the officer to do it, settling back into his chair and letting his attention return to his crows. The ones flying above Sophia's fleet circled, unable to get too close because the men of Ishjemme knew to shoot at them when they did. He didn't need to get close, though, to see the ships cutting through the water, sending up spray as they headed for Ashton.

How long had it taken to get to this point? How many pieces had he had to move into place to bring this about? His last invasion had been glorious, but the truth was that it had been little more than an overture, an opening act. It had been a necessary move to set the next phase in motion, and if the Master of Crows had calculated that correctly...

"Clancel," he said. "I have messages. Bring paper."

He waited for it, and then started to write orders in a neat, precise hand. Landing points, timings, expected outcomes. The orders would shift as his crows told him more of events, but by this point, the general course of things was flowing as surely as a river.

"Take them to the commanders," he said. "Tell them to begin."

His crows showed him other things beside the mass of ships. They showed him an empty cell in the basement of a townhouse. They showed him the spot where an ancient fountain was crumbling into dust. They showed him the space where the angry leaders of Stonehome were even now gathering a small group of chasers to bring back those who had left without asking. To another man, those might have looked like minor things. Even after he had

146

explained the game to Clancel, he was sure that the officer would not understand what they meant.

They meant a battle that would eclipse those that had gone before. They meant a tipping point, a moment that would no doubt be written about again and again in the years to come, looking for its causes. The Master of Crows wondered if any of them would understand his role in the war and the violence that would come.

Probably not, but the truth was that it didn't matter. All that mattered was that the battle was coming, in death after death with no would-be protector there to shield the island kingdom from him now. The Master of Crows would feast on the battle to come, and in the aftermath, he would sweep through the space it left.

It would be the greatest meal that the crows had ever had. The carnage would be spectacular, the energy produced incalculable. Perhaps, just perhaps, it would even prove to be enough.

CHAPTER TWENTY NINE

The townhouse had a long stretch of garden to the rear, and Angelica toured it, taking in the scents of the flowers there, admiring the small pond set to the rear with its lilies and its dragonflies.

A servant approached with a goblet of wine set on a silver tray. The servant was a woman a few years older than Angelica, innocuous enough looking with her medium-brown hair and slight frame, plain dark dress, and refusal to look up from the ground as she walked. She was so diffident that Angelica could barely see anything of her features. The goblet was a delicate copper thing, set with a design around it of green thorns.

"Do all assassins announce their presence so readily?" Angelica asked, very carefully tipping out the contents of the goblet onto the grass.

The so-called servant's demeanor shifted imperceptibly then, as she looked Angelica squarely in the eye. Something harder crept in beneath the rest of her expression, changing what had seemed like just a foolish servant into something that looked more like a snake getting ready to strike.

"Only when we are sent for. The first task is done. You requested my presence?"

Requested was the wrong word for it. Angelica had demanded it, required it, commanded it. Yet, when there was a murderer of this caliber standing in front of her, it didn't pay to be picky about these things.

"You are not what I expected," Angelica said. "What do I call you?"

The woman shrugged. "Call me Rose. And *you* of all people should know that being anything but what people expect can be useful, my lady."

There was something about her expression then that said she saw through all the carefully crafted outer layers of Angelica's façade, to what lay beneath. It was disconcerting, especially since this was the first time she'd met the assassin face to face like this. There was always the thin thread of fear that worried Angelica that she might not leave this meeting alive.

"You have a task for me," Rose said.

"I *had* a task for you," Angelica said.

"Two targets, in a guarded castle, in a place I do not know," the assassin replied. "And you sent another to do the job: an amateur whose bumbling only made things harder. These things take time, my lady. Especially when you were the one to interrupt me for another matter."

Angelica had to admit that she had handled that part well.

"You're right," she said. "I have no quarrel with you, Rose."

The assassin shrugged. "I have no quarrel with anyone. It's a foolish motive for killing. There's no profit in it."

"And for enough gold you would kill anyone?" Angelica asked.

The other woman looked at her as if it were foolish even to ask the question. "The gold is proportionate to the difficulties involved, of course. As I said, the matter of the sisters is a particularly tricky one."

Angelica suspected that she was just trying to push her price up a little further, but she let that go. When it came to getting rid of Sophia, the price didn't matter.

"Did you just call me here to talk to me?" Rose asked. "That would be a dangerous game, wanting to know me by sight, wasting my time, but there have been those who played it."

"I take it they are mostly dead?" Angelica asked.

"Mostly," the assassin agreed with a nod. "Although I'll admit that you interest me enough to make an exception, my lady."

Angelica wasn't sure if the interest of an assassin was exactly something to crave, but it seemed to be intended as a compliment, and in one way at least, Angelica supposed that she could see similarities with this woman: they were both willing to reach out and take what they wanted, for one thing, and neither of them was afraid to kill.

"Do you want me to return to my work with the sisters?" she asked.

Angelica considered for a moment, then shook her head. "Not yet. I have a matter that might fall more *easily* within your remit."

If the assassin was angered by that small insult, she showed no sign of it. "I was able to get in here without being observed," she said. "I performed the task you set. I could have killed you easily if I had wished to do so. What is this task of yours, my lady?"

"I would like Rupert killed." There was a risk in just saying the words, because Rupert had spies of his own, people who gave him information out of fear, or greed, or loyalty to the crown he would never be able to live up to.

The assassin was silent for several seconds. "I see," she said at last. "You do not set simple tasks. First the sisters and now this?"

"First this," Angelica corrected her. "But the sisters too."

"Why do you want Prince Rupert dead?" Rose asked. Her hand snaked out, catching Angelica's arm, making her wince as she touched some of the bruises Angelica had so carefully covered over with powder. "Ah, I see."

"You see less than you think," Angelica snapped. "I'm not some wife tired of her husband's whoring and drunkenness."

"You're not a wife at all, just yet," the assassin pointed out.

If it had been someone else, Angelica might have slapped them for that.

"Have a care," she said.

"Oh, I'm always careful," Rose replied. "Which is why I'll tell you now that it will not be easy."

Anger flashed in Angelica then. "Is *anything* easy for you?" she demanded. "The sisters weren't easy. Rupert isn't easy. What are you waiting for? Me to ask you to slay a babe in arms?"

"Had I wished to kill you here, *that* would have been easy," Rose said. "I would not have poisoned the wine. I would have put poison on the stem of the cup, for the moment when you poured it away."

Angelica resisted the urge to wipe her hand frantically on her dress. If there had been such a poison, she would already be dead.

"Will you do this thing or not?" Angelica asked.

"Oh, I'll do it," Rose assured her.

"Good. Although not immediately. Not until Rupert and I are married where everyone can see us. Not until there can be no doubt."

Rose nodded. "I understand. Of course, I should probably warn you that a crown prince dropping dead on his wedding night will probably raise suspicions, and it is the kind of situation where no expense will be spared in hunting down the killer."

"That is why you have just helped to provide one," Angelica said.

"Ah," the assassin replied. "I see." She nodded. "Everything will be as you wish. And my payment…"

"Will be more than generous," Angelica assured her. It was one circumstance where she wouldn't even betray her employee. It was better not to upset assassins, as a rule. Rose turned to go.

Angelica again resisted the urge to wipe her hands on her dress, but only just. She watched the assassin go instead, thinking about how things were unfolding. The situation was becoming complex; she hoped that her most recent move would help her to simplify it.

"It would be better if Sophia were dead," Angelica whispered to herself, but that would come soon enough. It would remove the threat she posed, both by who she was and what she meant to Sebastian. A knife in the middle of war was not so hard to arrange. Perhaps she would not even need to pay the assassin for it.

After that, the main challenge to the throne would be removed. Rupert would ascend, if he did all that Angelica had primed him to do. He would marry her, crown her as his queen…

And if she were the empty-headed noble girl she pretended to be, that might be enough for Angelica, but it wasn't. It wasn't even close to enough.

"I'm done trusting men to *give* me power," she said to the water of the pond. She'd heard stories of witches who could see the future using nothing more than the flat surface of such a pool. Angelica needed no magic, though, just the will to make the future that she wanted for herself.

She trailed her fingers through the water, thinking through what it had taken to get to this point. Sebastian had been her first move in the game. Marrying him was meant to secure her ties to the throne and put her in a position where she could have pushed aside Rupert for the throne by simply showing the world what he was. Sebastian had proved just how unreliable he was, though. He didn't have it in him to do what was needed, and his feelings for Sophia…

"She *will* die," Angelica reassured herself. "She will."

Now there was Rupert, who had the ambition, but far too many dangerous edges to his personality. Angelica had briefly entertained the idea that they might live as king and queen, but the truth was that he was too dangerously unpredictable for that. So he was going to die, too.

It would leave Angelica as queen over all of it.

Of course, Rose had been right: a situation benefiting her so clearly would only arouse suspicion. That was why she had chosen to have the assassin release Sebastian, rather than keeping him for her plaything. That part would come in time, when he was reviled by the people for "murdering" the king, and safely locked away in a tower somewhere.

As a plan, it had its dangers. Rupert might survive. He might learn what Angelica was trying to do. He might fail to do all the things that Angelica anticipated of him first, leaving them both at the nonexistent mercy of the Dowager. Angelica liked to try to contain all the possible outcomes of a situation like this, but the truth was that there were some circumstances where it was impossible to make certain of everything. The best that she could do was to set things in motion and adapt as necessary.

She wanted to believe that it would be good, though.

"I will be queen soon," she told herself, and the country would be a better place for it. It wouldn't be shackled to the injustices of the past or under the thumb of a madman, as it would be with Rupert. It wouldn't be torn apart to put people under the control of those with magic, as Sophia might do.

Instead, it would be run as it ought to be run, by someone who understood the play of power in the country and the personalities of the nobles who mattered. People might mutter at first about her ascent to the throne, but once Angelica had been there a year, they would understand that she had always been the best choice for it. Her rule would be both peaceful and stable.

Of course, before any of that could happen, there were people who needed to die.

Angelica had already made arrangements for Rupert.

The assassin could deal with Sophia if Endi couldn't improve his efforts.

And, assuming Angelica had said all the right things to Rupert, the Dowager herself would soon be a memory.

CHAPTER THIRTY

Rupert waited in his mother's chambers, palms sweating, fingers fidgeting with his sword belt as he sat there. He'd never felt quite like this before. Oh, he'd felt angry and nervous and uncomfortable plenty of times, but he'd never felt this kind of self-doubt, never sat there wondering if he was about to do the right thing.

Then again, he'd never been about to kill his mother before.

"You need to do this," he said. "You have to do this."

"Have to do *what*, Rupert?" his mother demanded, coming in with precise steps. Her guards shut the door behind her. Clearly she wanted to be able to rebuke him without having to maintain all the propriety of a queen. "What are you doing here?"

"Can I not have come to see my mother?" Rupert demanded, standing.

"No," the Dowager said. "You can't; not when you are currently supposed to be on a ship to one of my dependencies."

Rupert bit back his anger at that. His mother had tried to send him away. She'd tried to get rid of him so she could give her throne to Sebastian.

"I chose not to go," he said.

"Then you're choosing both to risk your mother's anger and defy your queen," his mother shot back. "And my reports tell me that you *were* on the ship. So you didn't just defy me, you tried to trick me."

"I sent a soldier along with Sir Quentin Mires to vouch for him."

"Then Mires will die for it," his mother said. She stood and moved to one of the room's windows. "You'll be lucky if I don't have *you* tried for your defiance, too."

Rupert stood to follow her. Despite what he'd come there to do, a part of him still wanted to work this out. He wanted his mother to give him what should have been his all along.

"You're being unreasonable," he said.

"Be very careful, Rupert," his mother replied. "Or you will find out just how unreasonable I can be."

She was going to threaten him here, now? Why could his mother not just show him the love that he was due as her son? Another mother wouldn't have put him in this position, wouldn't have tried to take everything away from him.

"Where is your brother?" she demanded. "I told you before that you were to release him before you left."

"Sebastian is where I left him," Rupert said. "He will *remain* where I left him."

His mother's expression darkened. "I promise you, Rupert, that before you leave this room, you will tell me where my son is."

"I'm your son too!" Rupert shouted back at her. "I'm your *eldest* son. I'm the one who should have inherited. I'm the one who didn't try to run away with… with some…"

"With Alfred and Christina Danse's eldest daughter," his mother supplied.

That made Rupert pause, his eyes widening in shock.

"So you see, Rupert, I know more about what is going on here than you ever could. That is why I am the one who gets to make the decisions here."

"Decisions like cutting me off!" Rupert snapped. He couldn't accept that. If his mother knew all that she did, why would she ever agree to Sebastian being her heir? It made no sense. It was just an insult.

"You are a man without any self-control," his mother said. Rupert saw her shake her head. "No, you are not even a man. You are a boy who never bothered to grow up when he should have."

"I am everything a man should be," Rupert insisted. He'd commanded men, he'd seduced women. He'd fought and he'd killed, made decisions that had fought off an invasion. He'd experienced more of what the world had to offer than most people managed in a lifetime.

His mother laughed at that, actually laughed. "You're as far from it as I can imagine, Rupert. Goddess knows I tried my best with you, but I failed. I let you have your head too much, and you turned into… well, into *this*."

She was speaking about him as if he were some horse that she'd tried to train and had now decided was only ready for the knacker's yard.

"What happened to you, Rupert?" she asked. "I did my best for you."

"As I remember it," Rupert said, "you were hardly there for most of it."

He tried to think back to when he'd been a child, and he could remember the endless succession of nannies and tutors far more easily than he could remember any time with his mother.

"Because I was busy trying to make sure that we weren't all killed by our enemies!" his mother snapped back. "We had only just come out of the civil wars. Your father was dead, lost in a stupid battle that he should have avoided, but—"

"Don't talk about my father like that!" Rupert shouted back.

His mother walked over to a portrait on the wall, from which his father stared down, looking every inch the king he'd been. How much time had Rupert spent trying to live up to that image, being strong, not letting the lower orders impinge on his station?

"You idolize your father, Rupert?" she said.

"He was a good man, a strong man," Rupert said. "You wouldn't have married him otherwise."

His mother snorted at that. "As if I got a choice in who I married. But yes, he was both of those things. And they killed him for it. You say I wasn't around for you as a boy? Well, who was around for *me*?"

"I..." Rupert didn't know what his mother was talking about.

"While you were growing up, I had to make decisions that reshaped this kingdom. I had to decide to ally with the Church of the Masked Goddess. I had to make deals with the Assembly of Nobles. I had to kill the traitors whose very presence threatened our kingdom, and I had to make those decisions *alone*. I had to make them because your father, foolish man that he was, had gone and gotten killed."

Rupert stayed silent. How dare his mother blame his father for all this? How dare she claim that it was his fault that Rupert had grown up without any of the warmth of human contact? How *dare* she?

"And I tried to do my best with you, Rupert," she said. "I gave you the finest tutors, the best sword masters. I gave you a post in my army when you did not deserve it, all the money you could wish for, endless patience with your indiscretions. I gave you advantages that no one else has had, and you threw them away."

"They were mine by right!" Rupert said.

"They were yours because I'd fought for them," his mother shot back. "Because I'd made decisions that—"

"They were the wrong decisions!" Rupert said. "You've spent my life complaining about all the compromises you've had to make, but why make them if they were so bad? You killed the nobles who opposed you, so why not kill the rest too? Why not be bold? Why be a coward about it?"

"You've gone too far, Rupert," his mother said, and now her voice was cold with anger.

"I will always go as far as I need to," Rupert said. "I *saved* this kingdom by being strong, but even then you and Sebastian whined that I was being too cruel, that the lives of the peasants mattered. You never even thanked me!"

The silence that followed seemed to echo with everything that had gone before.

"So this is what's going to happen," his mother said. "You're going to go, and you're going to do it now. My guards are going to take you down to the docks this time, where a ship to the Near Colonies will be waiting. I will not be defied. You will tell me where your brother is, and you will leave in disgrace where you could not leave before with a modicum of dignity."

Rupert shook his head. "No, I won't."

"You don't get a choice," his mother snapped. "You'll go, or I'll have you dragged there!"

"I won't go," Rupert shouted. There was a knife in his hand now, clenched so tight that his knuckles whitened. He'd come here to do this, but now that it was time, it wasn't as easy as it should have been. He'd killed so many people, but this, this was hard.

"What do you think you're going to do with that, Rupert?" his mother demanded. "You're a foolish boy, playing at being a man. Put it down now."

Rupert lowered it, but didn't let go.

"Put it down, tell me where my son is, and then—"

"*I* am your son!" Rupert bellowed.

Rupert stabbed her then, and it wasn't something he decided; he just did it. The blade slid into her flesh so easily, came out wet, and he slid it in again. He heard his mother gasp with it as he struck at her, all the anger of the years before coming out in one big rush. He stabbed her again because she wasn't falling yet, because she clawed at him and gripped at him and he wanted her to just stop.

She fell back, collapsing to the floor, her chest still rising and falling, but slowly now. Her eyes stared up at the ceiling, and through the hot wetness of his tears, Rupert saw the moment when they glazed over.

The knife in his hand was wet with blood, and it took him a moment to realize where it must all have come from, and what he'd just done.

"Oh, Goddess," he said, and fell to his hands and knees, struggling not to throw up. Ordinarily, death didn't bother him, but this… this was beyond anything else he'd done.

Distantly, he heard a booming sound, and it took Rupert a moment to realize that it was the sound of guards banging on the door. He thought quickly, standing to one side of the opening, then calling out.

"Help! We need some help here!"

The two men all but broke the door open then, standing there staring as they saw what Rupert had done. He couldn't blame them, but he reacted quicker than they did, his knife taking the first of them through the throat.

The second of them turned to him, reaching for his sword. Rupert was on him then, stabbing without precision, but with all the desperation that came from knowing what would happen if he did not. The man grabbed at his wrist, and Rupert hit him with his other hand. He felt the guard's grip weaken, and Rupert stabbed him, down through the shoulder, into the lung and out. He watched the man collapse, and then stared at the scene he'd created.

There was blood everywhere. Blood on the men he'd killed, blood on his mother, blood pooling on the floor in slicks of it that threatened to spread out and cover everything. There was blood on the knife Rupert held, and he wiped it on his shirt, only adding to the blood that was already there.

"What have I done?" he asked aloud. "What have I done?"

His tears were still falling, blurring the world around him into a shapeless mass of red. He didn't know what to do next. He only knew that he needed to get away.

So he turned and ran. Not caring about the blood that covered him, not caring who saw him do it, not caring about anything except putting that scene as far away as possible.

His mother was dead.

He was king now.

And everything was about to change

.

A KISS FOR QUEENS
(A Throne for Sisters—Book Six)

"Morgan Rice's imagination is limitless. In another series that promises to be as entertaining as the previous ones, A THRONE OF SISTERS presents us with the tale of two sisters (Sophia and Kate), orphans, fighting to survive in a cruel and demanding world of an orphanage. An instant success. I can hardly wait to put my hands on the second and third books!"
--Books and Movie Reviews (Roberto Mattos)

The new #1 Bestselling epic fantasy series by Morgan Rice!

In A KISS FOR QUEENS (A Throne for Sisters—Book Six), it is time for Sophia to come into her own. It is time for her to lead an army, to lead a nation, to step up and be the commander of the most epic battle the realm may ever see. Her love, Sebastian, remains imprisoned and set to be executed. Will they reunite in time?

Kate has finally freed herself from the witch's power, and is free to become the warrior she was meant to be. Her skills will be tested in the battle of her life, as she fights at her sister's side. Will the sisters save each other?

The Queen, furious at Rupert and Lady D'Angelica, exiles him and sentences her to execution. But they just may have their own agenda.

And all of this converges in an epic battle that will decide the future of the crown—and the fate of the realm—forever.

A KISS FOR QUEENS (A Throne for Sisters—Book Six) is book #6 in a dazzling new fantasy series rife with love, heartbreak, tragedy, action, adventure, magic, swords, sorcery, dragons, fate and heart-pounding suspense. A page turner, it is filled with characters that will make you fall in love, and a world you will never forget.

Book #7 in the series will be released soon.

"[A Throne for Sisters is a] powerful opener to a series [that] will produce a combination of feisty protagonists and challenging circumstances to thoroughly involve not just young adults, but adult fantasy fans who seek epic stories fueled by powerful friendships and adversaries."
--Midwest Book Review (Diane Donovan)

Books by Morgan Rice

THE WAY OF STEEL
ONLY THE WORTHY (Book #1)

A THRONE FOR SISTERS
A THRONE FOR SISTERS (Book #1)
A COURT FOR THIEVES (Book #2)
A SONG FOR ORPHANS (Book #3)
A DIRGE FOR PRINCES (Book #4)
A JEWEL FOR ROYALS (BOOK #5)
A KISS FOR QUEENS (BOOK #6)

OF CROWNS AND GLORY
SLAVE, WARRIOR, QUEEN (Book #1)
ROGUE, PRISONER, PRINCESS (Book #2)
KNIGHT, HEIR, PRINCE (Book #3)
REBEL, PAWN, KING (Book #4)
SOLDIER, BROTHER, SORCERER (Book #5)
HERO, TRAITOR, DAUGHTER (Book #6)
RULER, RIVAL, EXILE (Book #7)
VICTOR, VANQUISHED, SON (Book #8)

KINGS AND SORCERERS
RISE OF THE DRAGONS (Book #1)
RISE OF THE VALIANT (Book #2)
THE WEIGHT OF HONOR (Book #3)
A FORGE OF VALOR (Book #4)
A REALM OF SHADOWS (Book #5)
NIGHT OF THE BOLD (Book #6)

THE SORCERER'S RING
A QUEST OF HEROES (Book #1)
A MARCH OF KINGS (Book #2)
A FATE OF DRAGONS (Book #3)
A CRY OF HONOR (Book #4)
A VOW OF GLORY (Book #5)
A CHARGE OF VALOR (Book #6)
A RITE OF SWORDS (Book #7)
A GRANT OF ARMS (Book #8)
A SKY OF SPELLS (Book #9)

A SEA OF SHIELDS (Book #10)
A REIGN OF STEEL (Book #11)
A LAND OF FIRE (Book #12)
A RULE OF QUEENS (Book #13)
AN OATH OF BROTHERS (Book #14)
A DREAM OF MORTALS (Book #15)
A JOUST OF KNIGHTS (Book #16)
THE GIFT OF BATTLE (Book #17)

THE SURVIVAL TRILOGY
ARENA ONE: SLAVERSUNNERS (Book #1)
ARENA TWO (Book #2)
ARENA THREE (Book #3)

VAMPIRE, FALLEN
BEFORE DAWN (Book #1)

THE VAMPIRE JOURNALS
TURNED (Book #1)
LOVED (Book #2)
BETRAYED (Book #3)
DESTINED (Book #4)
DESIRED (Book #5)
BETROTHED (Book #6)
VOWED (Book #7)
FOUND (Book #8)
RESURRECTED (Book #9)
CRAVED (Book #10)
FATED (Book #11)
OBSESSED (Book #12)

About Morgan Rice

Morgan Rice is the #1 bestselling and USA Today bestselling author of the epic fantasy series THE SORCERER'S RING, comprising seventeen books; of the #1 bestselling series THE VAMPIRE JOURNALS, comprising twelve books; of the #1 bestselling series THE SURVIVAL TRILOGY, a post-apocalyptic thriller comprising three books; of the epic fantasy series KINGS AND SORCERERS, comprising six books; of the epic fantasy series OF CROWNS AND GLORY, comprising 8 books; and of the new epic fantasy series A THRONE FOR SISTERS. Morgan's books are available in audio and print editions, and translations are available in over 25 languages.

Morgan loves to hear from you, so please feel free to visit www.morganricebooks.com to join the email list, receive a free book, receive free giveaways, download the free app, get the latest exclusive news, connect on Facebook and Twitter, and stay in touch!